Leveled in London

The House Sitters Cozy Mysteries

Book 2

SCARLETT MOSS

Abby Moss Publishing

Leveled in London, The House Sitters Cozy Mysteries Book Two- Scarlett Braden

Copyright © 2020 Scarlett Braden

All rights reserved. Printed in the United States of America. No part of this book may be used or reproduced in any manner whatsoever without written permission except in the case of brief quotations embodied in critical articles or reviews.

For information contact :
Scarlett Braden at ScarlettBraden@gmail.com

The scanning, uploading and distribution of this book via the Internet or any other means without the permission of the publisher is illegal and punishable by law. Please purchase only authorized electronic or physical editions, and do not participate in or encourage electronic piracy of copyrighted materials. Your support of the author's rights is appreciated.

This is a work of fiction. Names, characters, places, and incidents either are the product of the author's imagination or are used fictitiously, and any resemblance to actual persons, living or dead, business establishments, events, or locales is entirely coincidental.

Chapter One

"Frankly, my dear, that didn't go at all like I expected it would," Alen Arny said to his wife of just shy of seventeen years.

"Isn't that what makes a good adventure, a great mystery, a fabulous experience?" Joan asked.

"True. I suppose without some suspense, intrigue, and a shady character or two, it would be excruciatingly routine."

"Since we have a four and a half-hour train ride ahead of us, why don't you tell me what exactly didn't go as you expected for our first house-and pet-sitting gig?"

"Well, first of all, I thought the whole idea of quitting our jobs and traveling the world living in other people's houses and taking care of their pets meant we were getting away from a life of crime."

"Alen!" Joan whisper-yelled. "If that's overheard, people

will get the wrong idea!"

"Should we stand up and introduce ourselves?" Alen asked, and his facial expression looked absolutely serious.

Fortunately, Joan knew her husband well enough to know that he would never do that; he might expect her to, but he wouldn't. Alen was a retired sheriff from Corpus Christi, Texas, also a retired marine, and Joan recently retired from her twenty-five-year tenure as a 911 dispatch operator. They were en route from their first international house-sitting job in Edinburgh, Scotland, to their next gig, in London. Joan decided to ignore the silly question and press on with the discussion at hand. It was a debriefing of sorts, in her mind. Leaving one job, one city, one set of people, and a darling dog behind and preparing for the next.

"Let's think about this. We expected to be tourists and see all the iconic and interesting things," she said.

"And we did."

"We expected to try new and exotic foods."

"That we did."

"We expected to learn new cultures."

"Aye, we did."

"We wanted to try new things."

"We did. But I didn't want to be investigating a crime. I wanted to leave that behind. That's not something new," Alen protested.

"But it was new for me! And you did learn something new. You learned to cook."

"True."

"And, because we worked to help the neighbor next door with his sticky situation and discover who was blackmailing him, we made some new friends."

"Yeah, that's true too. But if it's all the same to you, I prefer to not have any friends in London. Okay? What does my research ninja wife have on the schedule for us in London? And what do we know about these homeowners?"

"To be honest, Edinburgh was so fascinating and there were so many unique things to do there, that I was afraid London was going to be quite the snoozefest. But I was wrong! We'll be there for twenty-four days, and every single day of my calendar is booked with amazingness."

"Joan, I don't think amazingness is really a word," Alen pointed out.

"It is now. I just created it, because it should be a word. Anyway, the homeowners are Addison and Layne Cotton. They're Americans like us and are taking their first trip back to the U.S. in five years. I'm not sure how old they are, but they seem very nice from the emails we've exchanged. This house sit is going to be a little different. They have two dogs, goldendoodles, named Mr. Darcy and Elizabeth Bennett."

"You have got to be kidding me, right now. Aren't you?" Alen asked.

"Nope, not at all. What's wrong, I think those names are cute?"

"I just hope they have some shorter nicknames. A dog with legs that long will be half way to Ireland before you finish calling them back!"

Joan laughed. "I see your point; I imagine they do. We'll find out shortly. Anyway, the first floor of their home is a shop. A consignment thrift shop, called Love It or Thrift It. Part of our duties while we are here is to keep the shop open while they're gone."

"Seriously? Two large dogs and a store to run? That won't leave much time for exploring the city, and definitely no time for crime solving! So, no sticking our noses into the neighbor's business this time around, agreed?"

"We won't be the only ones working the store. Addison and Layne's best friends, another retired American couple, will work half of every day the store is open. They have agreed to work around our sightseeing schedule. The store is open from 10 to 8 six days a week. So, if we have an afternoon or evening tour, they will work closing, and if it's a daytime activity, they'll work mornings. They prefer to work the mornings. I'm guessing they are older and like to go to bed early. So, I carefully planned our schedule where they will only work two evening shifts a week."

"Look at you! You could be a cruise director. Mrs. Arny, I never knew you were a scheduling whiz, a planner extraordinaire. Will we be able to take the dogs to the parks every morning like we did in Edinburgh?"

"I don't think so. London is much bigger, and we won't have a car this time. We'll be relying on public transportation."

"Bummer, that was nice," he lamented.

"We'll still go to the parks; we just can't take the dogs."

"It doesn't sound like we're going to have much time to breath. Can we agree that, if for some reason we find ourselves in the vicinity of a crime, we duck our heads and run the other way?"

"What are the chances of that happening? It would be like lightening striking twice."

"Sweetheart, scientists estimate the earth is struck by lightning a hundred times every second. It most assuredly does strike in the same place twice. Please, please, please, I beg of you, don't tempt fate."

"Fine. I had fun with that case. I liked it. And it's new for me. So, if crime finds us, I'll play detective and you can play in the kitchen. Or whatever other thing you want to learn. Shall I search to see if there are bagpipe lessons you could take?"

Leveled in London

"First you want me to fly wearing a bare-chested hunk in a kilt apron and now you want me to learn to play bagpipes? You promised to never try to change me."

"You're right. I did. But you're awfully sexy in that apron. Especially with a wooden spoon in your hand too."

They both laughed and spent the rest of the trip going over all the tours and places Joan wanted to visit while they were in London. They also agreed that they needed to make a change in their diet or they would outgrow their clothes. They made a pact to eat a salad for at least one meal a day while in London. They would have just less than twenty-four hours with Addison and Layne to show them all they needed to know about the house, dogs, and shop before they left the next day. Once they arrived in London, they were likely in for the busiest twenty-four hours of their stay.

Alen was amazed that before they could leave the King's Cross train station, Joan found a photo opportunity at Platform 9 3/4 from the Harry Potter books. It was an interestingly staged platform with a baggage trolley that disappeared into a brick wall. It seemed that no matter where they went, Joan found something interesting to memorialize with a photo. She learned in Edinburgh how to make a video of her travel photos and her plan was to make a new video in each place they visited. Alen chuckled to himself at the memory that almost half of all the pictures from Edinburgh were men wearing kilts, most playing the bagpipes.

Joan wondered what she would find in London to photograph that would be as interesting as those kilt-clad, pipe-playing men.

SCARLETT MOSS

Chapter Two

ALEN AND JOAN HAILED AN iconic black hackney taxi at the train station. Joan gave the driver the address they would call home for the next three weeks, on York Street in the area of London called Twickenham. It was a Friday afternoon and the traffic was thick. It took about an hour to get from King's Cross to the house. They traveled above and through the center of Regent's Park, and Alen noticed a big green dome to the right. He asked the driver what it was and the driver told him that was the famous Madame Tussaud's wax museum.

"Are we going there, Sweetheart?" Alen asked Joan.

"Of course, Honey! We can take photos with famous people there."

"For your video."

"Yes. I suspect this video may be even longer than the last. Except a lot of places here don't allow photos, so who knows what we'll capture!"

The driver stopped in front of a street long, four-story building with storefronts on the first floor with shop windows and obviously living quarters above. The awning over the store window on the end said Love It or Thrift It. This was home. Before the driver could remove their luggage from the *boot* or trunk, a couple came out of the store.

"Welcome! I'm Addison, and this is Layne. Let us help you with your luggage."

Once they were inside the store, Joan noticed a set of stairs on the far-left side of the store that went upstairs. There was a glass wall overlooking the shop and they could see the two dogs waiting impatiently peering down from the glass wall. There was a short gate across the top of the stairs to keep the dogs in the living quarters.

When Addison opened the gate, the two dogs sat and waited for everyone to clear the top of the stairs. Joan could tell it was hard for them. Their whole bodies were wiggling from tail to head, but their butts were firmly planted to the floor. They were identical. One was slightly smaller but it was almost impossible to tell them apart. But Joan figured it out even before Addison had a chance to introduce them.

"Aren't you two beautiful, and very mannerly! You must be Elizabeth Bennett," Joan cooed. When her name was said, one dog stood up but waited for Joan to pet her. "And you must be Mr. Darcy!" The second dog stood and she petted him.

"How did you know which was which?" Alen asked puzzled.

"Look at their collars, silly," Joan answered.

Alen looked. Sure enough, Elizabeth had a pink rhinestone encrusted collar, and Mr. Darcy's was blue with no rhinestones. He then petted them both. Then Alen and Joan looked around them. They were standing in a contemporary open space kitchen flooded with light from the store windows on the front of the building. Joan realized immediately they would need to be dressed before venturing to the kitchen in the morning as one could see in from the street level because of the uncovered shop windows. There was also a restroom and another door that they were now following Addison through.

Alen had to ask. "Do you have shorter nicknames for the dogs? I'm thinking if you need to call them quickly."

Addison laughed, "Yeah, we hardly ever call them by their full names. It's more a parlor trick. We call them Darcy and Lizzy usually."

"Oh, good. I could just see one getting away and, before we could get them back, they would be on their way to the grassy lands of Ireland."

"Actually, I was quite impressed with the amount of green space on our drive here from the train station. I envisioned a thousands-year-old bustling city would be all pavement and concrete," Joan said.

"London has done green space well. There is a lot of it, and trees. I was surprised by how many trees there are when we got here," Addison added.

"We use that area during the work day for something to eat or drink and the restroom. But through here are the living quarters."

They entered a beautifully decorated contemporary living room with another staircase at the back. Under the staircase was a wet bar, complete with sink, refrigerator and coffee pot. Joan was relieved. There was another door that looked like it might be an exit.

"This wet bar should have everything you need before and after hours. If you want to cook, that's only in the big kitchen, but I didn't think you would want to cook while you're here so we made other arrangements for you. That door there leads out to the back alley. The dog walkers will come in and out of that door."

"I thought I was going to have to be showered and dressed in the morning before coffee," Joan said.

"Oh no. And actually, there are electric shades you can lower on the shop windows if it makes you feel better. We sometimes do that on Sundays or holidays when we're closed all day, if we feel the need for privacy. I'll show you how to do that when we come back down."

Addison started up the next stairway. Lizzie and Darcy were following along behind. On the next floor were three bedrooms each with its own bathroom.

"There is another door here at the top of the stairs. We have a great dog-walking team and they have keys to the living area entrance from the alley. But if we are going to be gone, we usually close and lock this door, just for safety sake."

"Won't it be our responsibility to walk the dogs?" Joan asked.

"No. The walkers come every day at 7 a.m., 2 p.m., and 9 p.m. If you want to walk them, you're welcome to, and they would love an extra walk. But this is their routine, and our walkers count on that money. We didn't want to disrupt anyone's schedule. Oh yes, and we have a lady who comes every Friday and cleans the house and the shop. She comes during shop hours and doesn't have a key. Her name is Mrs. White. You'll like her. She's not very talkative but she does a great job."

They left the suitcases in one of the bedrooms that Addison said would be their room and then followed her up one more flight of stairs to the fourth floor. There was an office and a library on the final floor. The house was almost a polar opposite from the Clarke's house in Edinburgh. It was clean, contemporary, and well decorated with a more formal feel. Not like a museum, but not as cozy as the last house.

"Feel free to use the printer in the office, you can set your computers up in there if you like. Also, help yourself to the library. I admit it's not a typical English library. No leather bound first editions, no classics. We both read contemporary fiction."

"That's great! I read every night, but I had to convert to eBooks when we started traveling. No room in the suitcases for real books. But I still love holding a real print book. Thank you!" Joan said.

"Layne is manning the shop this afternoon, so let's go down for something to eat."

Alen and Joan expected to return to the kitchen, where Addison opened a cabinet and took out four large travel coffee cups with lids, and then kept going to the first floor.

"We're going to get something to eat. Do you want anything, Layne?" Addison called out. Layne answered from somewhere in the back of the store.

"I'm on my way to the front. Yes, bring me a snack back, please," he called out and then came into view.

Addison turned to Alen and Joan.

"On this block, we have a tea shop, an expresso bar, and a pub. The owners are all friends. We like the tea shop for breakfast. She has a daily selection of scones. The English have them for afternoon tea. We like them for breakfast. Oddly, the coffee shop has delectable desserts and all types of coffee. We usually hit them up for an afternoon carryover. Then the pub down the way is our go to for dinner. We've set up tabs with all of them. Whatever you order from them, we will pay for when we get back. Of course, you don't have to eat there, but we found it so convenient, and they have daily specials so the menu doesn't get stale."

"That's not necessary!" Alen said. "We usually pay to feed

ourselves. Since we are staying in your home, that's our expense," he explained.

"Yeah, we know that's normally how the house-sitting thing works. But you're also working in our business. So, this is not up for discussion," Layne replied.

"Are you up for coffee and dessert, or would you prefer a late lunch? We usually eat dinner after the shop closes at eight," Addison asked.

"Coffee and dessert," Alen and Joan said in unison.

"The Mug Shot Expresso Bar it is!" They left the store, turned to the left and walked down about four store fronts, passing the tea room, called The Tea's Knees.

"What a cute tea room," Joan said as they walked quickly by.

"Do you always bring your own cups with you?" Alen asked.

"Yes. London is doing away with single-serving throwaway containers. So, when you order a coffee or tea, you need your own cup if you want to take it with you. Otherwise, you're served in a china cup or glass and must finish it in the establishment. There are plenty of them in the cabinet. You'll get used to carrying one with you. Also, an umbrella, or what they call a *brolly* here."

"Sounds like backpacks are a good idea here," Joan commented.

"We have some you can borrow if you need them."

"We both have one, but thank you," Alen replied.

Addison pushed open the door that had The Mug Shot Expresso Bar stenciled on it.

"Hi, Addison. Are these your house sitters?"

"Yes. Summer Lane, this is Joan and Alen," Addison introduced them.

"Nice to meet you. What can I get you today? Today's treats are on the chalk board, they change daily," Summer explained.

Leveled in London

"It's nice to meet you too," Joan said, and Alen reached out to shake her hand.

"Banana Pecan English pudding sounds good and a cappuccino, please," Joan ordered.

"I'll have the same," Alen said.

"Make it a threesome," Addison teased and handed the four mugs to Summer. "I'll get one to take away for Layne when we're ready to go."

They sat at a table by the window to watch the traffic and people walking by, and Addison explained how the shop worked, promising to show them how the register worked before they went to dinner. Grace and Tommy Bell, the couple who would be working in the shop with them, were going to join them for dinner. They ate dessert, which Alen and Joan both loved and praised Summer for, and drank their cappuccinos. Addison had Summer make them fresh cappuccinos to go along with Layne's once she learned that Alen and Joan loved coffee as much as she did.

Love It or Thrift It was set up like a lovely home within the shop. They carried home decor items and furniture exclusively, so there were vignettes set up for all the rooms of a house with furniture, lamps, rugs, and knickknacks appropriate for each room. Joan and Alen were impressed that with the inventory being on consignment, each room setting seemed complete and looked like a designer planned each detail.

"That's my wife's secret power," Layne said when Joan commented on it. "She can put a room together and make it look like a million dollars no matter what she has to work with."

"It's a good thing we live out of a suitcase and I can't shop, or my checking account would be in real danger in here. It's all so lovely," Joan commented.

Before they knew it, it was time to close the shop and walk

down the street to The Ugly Shakespeare to meet Grace and Tommy and enjoy dinner with their hosts.

The conversation was lively as both of the couples wanted to know all about how Joan and Alen decided to become house sitters and how they enjoyed their stay in Scotland. By previous mutual agreement, they didn't mention the adventure of trying to solve a crime undercover in Edinburgh. Alen even seemed reluctant to mention his past as a sheriff as a dinner not unlike this one is what landed them in hot water before. The owner of the pub, Declan Burns, turned out to be good friends with Addison and Layne, too. He welcomed them warmly and said he looked forward to getting to know them during their stay.

Layne asked, "What does your family think about you doing this? I know our family sometimes acts like we moved to a remote island and abandoned them."

"We don't have any family," Joan said. Before she could finish, Tommy interrupted.

"Yeah, we've found a lot of expatriates say that. I get it. Sometimes I wish I didn't have family. But it always makes me wonder. Do they really not have family, or are they estranged from their family? And if they are estranged, why? Are they on the lam? Have they assumed new identities? Is one of them kidnapped?"

"Wow, you sound like you spent too much time in law enforcement," Alen said laughing. Tommy stared at him. He wasn't smiling.

Joan rushed to explain, "We are both only children whose parents died many years ago. We neither one have children. So, we don't have family. The house sits booking organizations conduct thorough background checks. We aren't serial killers, and Alen is not my hostage," she replied. She didn't sound like she was trying to convince them of anything, in fact, her tone sounded like she found the whole thing humorous.

"How about you? What does your family think, Tommy?" Alen asked.

"Oh. Me? I don't have any family," Tommy said. Grace laughed.

"We do have family. He's teasing you. I apologize. You'll learn he has an, um, sick and twisted sense of humor. Don't mind him," Grace said.

"I know," was all Alen said. But he looked at Tommy knowingly.

"The agencies aren't the only ones who can do background checks," Joan said.

Layne squirmed a bit in his seat.

SCARLETT MOSS

Chapter Three

THE NEXT MORNING, ALEN AND JOAN met Addison and Layne in the living room at 6:45 a.m. They drank a leisurely coffee together while the dog walkers took Lizzie and Darcy on their morning walk. When the dogs returned, they walked down to The Tea's Knees where Addison introduced them to the owner, Fern Scott. Addison bought an assortment of scones to take back to the shop for last minute instructions.

"Did you make plans for today?" Layne asked Alen and Joan.

"While we were in Edinburgh, we had a car, and we took Sherlock, the dog we were sitting with, to a different park every morning. We found we loved that. It was a great way to start the day. But London is so spread out and we hear the traffic is terrible, so we know we can't do that here. But we do want to at least visit the Royal parks. We thought we would start with the famous Hyde

Park today. We'll be back before you leave for the airport, though."

"We have a car too, and we thought of leaving it for you. But it's time for its maintenance and we didn't want to leave that for you. It's a lot that we are leaving you the dogs and the shop. So, we scheduled it to be in the shop while we're gone."

"Don't worry! It's not expected at all. Especially in a city like this with great public transportation," Joan said.

"Shoot! That reminds me, I almost forgot! Here, I got you both oyster cards," Addison said reaching into her purse and pulling out two plastic cards.

"Oyster cards?" Alen asked.

"Yes, you need them for the underground and the buses. I put two hundred dollars on each one. If you run out, you can top it up at a kiosk in any of the stations. Just remember, you have to swipe to get on, and swipe when you leave. You're billed for the length of your trip, but there is a daily maximum."

"Thank you, that's very generous. We don't know how to thank you, it seems like you've done too much," Joan protested but took the cards from Addison's outstretched hand.

"Just remember too, when you are on the escalator going down to the underground, always stand on the right side. The left side is for those walking, and Londoners will get quite miffed if you block their expedited passage," Layne explained.

"Thanks for letting us know. We want to be good guests here and not ruffle any feathers," Joan said.

Alen and Joan set off for Hyde Park to walk and explore while Addison and Layne finished their last-minute preparations for the trip. Grace and Tommy were working the shop in the morning, and Joan and Alen would begin their shop duties at three in the afternoon. They were confident they wouldn't have any problems as the shop was well organized and Addison's instructions were clear.

Leveled in London

They walked past Speaker's Corner in Hyde Park. There was a small crowd gathered listening to a man on his soap box, as Alen called it. Since 1866, on Sunday mornings, speakers would speak on whatever they were passionate about and people would gather to listen. Topics might be politics, global concerns, or any number of topics. Now, smaller crowds gathered and people would speak all through the week, but the crowds were typically smaller than on Sundays. They walked along the Serpentine Lake which divided the park into the two parks of Hype Park on one side and Kensington Gardens on the other. They were walking toward the Diana, Princess of Wales, Memorial Fountain. They chatted and held hands as they walked, except when Joan would stop to capture a photo for her planned London travel photo video.

"I was surprised at how young both Addison and Layne and Grace and Tommy are," Joan said.

"Me too. I thought you said Grace and Tommy are retired," Alen commented.

"I did. That's what Addison said. But it's also quite clear that money is plentiful for Addison and Layne too. I wish we'd had more time together to get the scoop," Joan said.

"Don't start. I swear, Joan, you are more curious than all my former deputies put together," Alen said playfully squeezing her hand.

"I'm not investigating, just curious is all," she insisted.

"I think we need to find you something new to get interested in. What kind of classes could we find for you? Knitting maybe?" Alen laughed, because the thought of his wife sitting and knitting seemed about as likely as Princess Diana walking out of the fountain in front of them. Joan just glared at him and didn't respond. But she was smiling, it was all in fun and she knew it.

After walking around Hyde Park, they opted to visit Dicken's

Tavern for lunch. Despite all the castles, palaces, parks, and attractions, Joan read that the pubs were some of the most iconic places to experience in London. They had an early light lunch and returned to the house to see Addison and Layne off. They left at 1:00 p.m. to catch their flight. The day went off without a hitch. After Addison and Layne left, Joan went to the spare room where their suitcases were stored. Inside her suitcase she pulled out the three things that she brought along to make each place feel like home. They had sold all of their belongings before leaving the States, and suitcase space was at a premium. But she brought along a framed picture from their wedding day and placed it on Alen's nightstand. And a table runner her coworkers gave her. It was in bright primary colors that she loved and had several diamonds in the center. The diamonds served to frame various species of frogs. Joan sold her frog collection before leaving, and this was one of few she brought along. Between the diamonds, she had affixed Alen's marine emblems, ribbons, and badges. And the third thing she brought along was the Mr. and Mrs. Frog salt and pepper shakers Alen gave her on their first anniversary. She placed the table runner and the shakers on the large glass table in the kitchen, and declared the house on York Street home for the time being. Then they relieved Grace and Tommy and told them they would see them on Monday.

    When they closed the shop at eight, they walked down to The Ugly Shakespeare for dinner.

    "What a perfect day this turned out to be," Alen said to Joan.

    "It was. I am going to miss going to a park each morning, but it just won't work. We'll get exercise on the walking tours, but it doesn't feel the same. Who would have thought we would get spoiled and into a new habit we aren't ready to abandon during our first house sit?"

    "I know. But I like this one. Working half a day is nice. It gives purpose to a day. I did kind of wonder what I would do all day. I'm still not adjusted to this retirement thing. Hunting for Ian's blackmailer did help fill the days and give me purpose. Even though I don't want to do that anymore."

"I understand, Honey. And you don't have to do it anymore."

"Do what anymore?" the owner of the pub, Declan, asked as he brought their dinner of two juicy hamburgers and fries, or *chips* as they were called in London.

"Investigate crimes," Alen answered. "I'm a retired sheriff, and I don't want to do that anymore."

"Can't blame you there," Declan said. "Enjoy your meal and let me know if I can get you anything else."

When they returned home after dinner, Lizzie and Darcy were just returning with the dog walker from their last walk of the day. As they did with their previous dog sit, they planned to spend the evening hours with the dogs, relaxing and watching TV. But Lizzie and Darcy weren't allowed on the furniture. They also seemed a little reserved this night, no doubt because their mom and dad left with suitcases. So, Alen and Joan sat in the floor, Alen petting and brushing Lizzie, and Joan brushing and petting Darcy. It was a quiet night.

"Mrs. Social Director, what's on the schedule for tomorrow? The shop is closed, right?"

"Right, it is. Tomorrow I thought we could go to Harrod's. Have lunch at the famous Nag's Head pub, take some photos and relax before we start a crazy busy week. And I figured we needed to be around for these guys a little more tomorrow. Say, did you program Grace and Tommy's phone numbers into our phones? That's who we're supposed to call if there is an emergency," Joan reminded him.

"No, I'll do that right now, but isn't Harrod's a department store? You hate shopping. Why are we going there?" Alen asked.

"Because it's famous. It's the biggest store in all of Europe. On a five-acre site, it has over a million square feet of shopping space with 330 departments."

"Wow. Okay. And this appeals to a non-shopper who can't buy anything because of suitcase space because?"

"They have great shopping bags. And it's famous!" she answered as though he was silly to not understand the concept.

"All I know is that if most men in the world knew that there was a department store with over a million square feet, they would have new fodder for nightmares. If I have to go, I'm thrilled my wife hates shopping as opposed to one who loves it. How long does it take to look at a million square feet of shoes and clothes and whatever else?"

"Put the phone numbers in our phones, please," was the only response he got.

Chapter Four

AT 6:30 ON SUNDAY MORNING, Joan was in her robe making coffee when someone knocked on the door that led to the back alley. It was not a soft knock, and she jumped even though Darcy and Lizzie were barking a split second before the rap on the door. It was the first time she heard the dogs bark.

"What on earth? Are the dog walkers this early? And the dogs don't bark at either of the two walkers who have come since we've gotten here," Joan said out loud even though there was no one to hear her. "What is it, pups? Or rather, I know what it is, but who is it?" Joan recovered from being frozen mid scoop in the can of coffee when there was a second knock. This one harder and louder than the first.

"I'm coming," she said. "Pups, hold on, let's see if it's someone who needs to be barked at or maybe a friend," she said as she clipped leashes on both dogs to hold them before opening the door.

Before she got to the door, Alen came down the stairs and asked, "What's going on?"

"I don't know, but I feel better that you're here," and she opened the door.

Standing on the other side of the door were two men in suits. They were middle-aged and looked very serious.

"Good morning, it's very early. How can I help you?" Joan asked, barely masking her peevishness at the early hour interruption to their day off.

"Mrs. Cotton?" one of the men asked.

"No. I'm sorry. She isn't home. Who might you be?"

"Is Mr. Cotton home?"

By now, Alen was also standing in the doorway. He smelled cops. Joan backed away from the door and led the dogs back into the room. They stopped barking but were tense. Their bodies were rigid, tails were not wagging, and they weren't about to sit down. They were ready to spring.

"We're the Arnys. The Cottons are out of town. We're the house sitters. What can we do to help you?" Alen asked.

"I'm DCI Sharp, and this is my partner DCI Fox with the City of London Police. May we come in?"

"Do you have credentials? Identification?" Alen asked.

Both men pulled warrant cards from their pockets and showed them to Alen.

"Come in, please. I apologize for our surprise. We've only been in London since Friday and aren't aware of the police procedures here. How can we help you?"

"We're looking for Mr. and Mrs. Cotton," the detective named Fox said, as he opened a small notebook and consulted it continuing, "Addison Cotton and Layne Cotton."

"As, I said, they are out of town. We are caring for the home, the dogs, and the business while they are away. Joan, sweetheart, go ahead and finish making the coffee, it will calm the dogs," Alen suggested.

"You said you arrived Friday?" Sharp asked.

"Yes, Friday afternoon," Alen answered.

"I see. You're American too?" Fox asked.

"Yes," Alen replied.

"What flight did you arrive on?" Fox asked.

"Come in have a seat, the coffee will be ready shortly. We came by train from Edinburgh."

"Do you still have your ticket stub?" Sharp asked after everyone had a seat in the living room. The dogs sat too.

"Yes, I'm sure we do. What's going on? Are we in trouble?"

"When exactly did the Cotton's leave and where are they now?"

"They left yesterday afternoon flying to the United States. They should be there now, but are probably sleeping given the time difference." Alen recognized the tactic and knew it was futile to ask more questions. The cops were the only ones asking the questions. He started to feel nervous.

"How can you reach them? Did they leave a phone number?"

"Just an email. We can try to email them. They are staying with a family member, I believe."

"Can you get us the email address, please? As well as your passports." Sharp was now asking all the questions.

"Yes, I'll get them," Joan answered. "Honey, hold the dogs, I'll be right back."

"Can I fix you officers some coffee?" Alen asked.

"No thank you." Sharp answered.

"In the United States law enforcement officers live on

coffee. I apologize, would you prefer tea?"

"Sir, are you making fun of us? Or law enforcers in general?" Fox asked.

"Oh no, neither! I was a sheriff before I retired. I was apologizing for the cultural difference. I understand Brits tend to drink more tea than we do."

Joan returned with the passports and a piece of paper with Addison's email address.

"I'm sorry this is all the information they left us. They're supposed to email us later today with a phone number," Joan explained.

Fox wrote down the information in his notebook, including the information on both Joan and Alen's passports.

"What is a phone number we can use to contact you?"

Joan gave them both of their phone numbers.

"Can I ask what this is about?" Alen asked.

"We need to talk to them about a murder yesterday."

"Murder?" Alen and Joan exclaimed simultaneously.

"Yes. A business competitor of the Cottons was found murdered in his consignment shop yesterday. The man's business partner said there might be some bad blood between him and the Cottons."

"Oh, my," Joan said. "Well, we were with the Cottons. I assure you they didn't murder anyone."

"Well, hold on sweetheart. It would depend on when the man was murdered. We weren't with them the whole time. Remember?"

"I can't give you any details, but you can see that it does look convenient that the Cottons left the country yesterday."

"But this trip was planned several weeks ago. I've known for two weeks that we would be house sitting for them. I'm sure you can check when they bought their tickets," Joan said. Alen just shook his head. This was looking bad. Very bad. So much for not getting in the middle of a crime investigation.

"If you hear from them, please let them know we need to speak with them immediately," Sharp said to Alen.

The inspectors stood and walked to the door.

"Of course, we will."

"How long are you supposed to be in London?" Fox asked.

"Until the 29th," Joan answered, once again holding tight on the dog's leashes. When the officers stood, so did the dogs.

"I'm sure we'll be in touch again," Sharp said as the two City of London Police inspectors left through the door.

"Joan, please email Addison right away. The sooner they contact the police the better! For them and for us."

"You can't honestly believe that while we were walking in the park, they killed someone, can you?"

"Sweetheart, my best friends were corrupt back home and I never saw it. Sadly, I believe people can do all kinds of things because I've seen it. And we really don't know anything about them at all."

"They seem like really nice people. Not murderers."

"You said yourself, it seems like they have a lot of money at their disposal. Do you think that comes from this thrift shop?"

"Well," Joan said taking a deep breath, "No, probably not. What should we do? Should we call Grace and Tommy?"

"No, not yet. Email Addison, hopefully, they will answer soon. I'm going to look online and see if there is any news about it."

There was a knock on the door. This time, it was a soft gentle knock and the dog's tails wagged. There was no barking. Joan took another deep breath.

"The dog walkers are here; I'll send them off and then email Addison."

Joan had not decided yet if this was going to be fun or if they somehow could be in jeopardy themselves. After she sent the email, she dressed and wondered, if something went wrong, if the Cottons didn't return or if they did and were arrested, what would they do with the dogs? They were due at another house-sitting gig the first of the month.

Joan went back to the living room and poured herself a long overdue cup of coffee. She checked to see if Addison had emailed her back. There was nothing.

Alen returned. Joan handed him a cup of coffee too. He was carrying his laptop. They sat down and he opened it.

"I found it. There aren't many details, but the man's name was River Read. He owned a consignment shop called Upcycled Kingdom. I guess it's a play on U.K., kind of catchy. They found him yesterday. The paper doesn't say when or how he died, just that he was found at his shop by his business partner. I guess it's too soon for more details than that, but at least it's something we can tell Addison and Layne."

"If we hear from them. I have a bad feeling about this, Alen."

"Don't worry, sweetheart. I agree, I don't think they are murderers. But if I was wanted for questioning in a foreign country and I was out of the country, I would think long and hard about returning. At least before the case was solved. It's sad but true, that cops would rather pin a crime on a foreigner than a local."

"I guess that's human nature. But where does that leave us?" Joan asked.

"I don't know."

The dogs returned, Joan thanked the walkers and told them they would likely be out for the 2 p.m. walk.

"Alen, honey, while you get dressed, I'll run over to The Tea's Knees and get some scones for breakfast. Then we can decide what to do next."

"Joan Michelle Arny, we are going to continue with our plans. We're going to Harrods, and we're going to have lunch in a famous English pub. And we are staying out of this!" Alen said emphatically.

"Well, Mr. Alen Wade Arny, we just may not have a choice about this. I think we are going to be in the middle of this whether we want to or not." Joan answered just as emphatically.

"Jumping sour biscuits, I'm afraid you may be right. I sure hope you're wrong, though!"

"Don't worry. I'll solve this one."

"Heaven help me! I want a blueberry scone, please," he said as she walked out the door.

SCARLETT MOSS

Chapter Five

"GOOD MORNING," FERN, THE OWNER of The Tea's Knees, greeted her when she walked through the door. She was busy helping a line of customers. Sunday mornings were obviously a busy time for her. But Joan didn't mind. It gave her time to look over the chalkboard menu and decide what she wanted. Alen requested blueberry, but it wasn't on the menu today. There were some exotic flavors offered. Her list was longer on Sunday than it had been yesterday. But Joan realized she wasn't in the mood to try something new today. As much as she hated to admit it, she was nervous. She felt almost shell-shocked. And she hated how much they had teased about crime-solving up to this point. It never occurred to her that she and Alen could wind up in literally in the middle of a crime, with absolutely no control over it. It reminded her of being a small child and thinking that washing dishes or vacuuming were fun. Until one had to do them with no choice. Then those things weren't fun anymore.

When it was her turn to order, Fern greeted her by name.

"Good morning, Joan. What can I get you today?"

"Wow, you're very busy today. I'll have two strawberry scones and two cinnamon scones, to go, please," Joan answered.

"You've got it. Four scones for takeaway. Anything else?"

"No, that will do today, thank you," Joan answered automatically. She still seemed in another world. But Fern didn't know her well enough yet to know that, and the tea room was busy enough to avoid a conversation.

~***~

Wandering around the 1,000,000 square feet of shopping space in Harrod's was a perfect way to try to forget the early morning visit from London's finest. And watching the email to hear back from Addison or Layne. Alen reminded Joan of the time difference and that they may sleep in after their long flight and time change. It was an amazing store to walk through, and though Joan knew their no shopping rule because of suitcase space, she really wanted one of those famous dark green shopping bags. She was delighted when they stumbled upon the coffee, tea, and chocolate department.

"Perfect! We can buy something here, get a shopping bag, and we have plenty of time to consume it before we fly," she announced as she walked over to the displays to decide on her purchases. Normally not a shopper and normally very frugal, this time she was looking for the biggest items she could buy. Because she wanted a big bag. Alen leaned against a post and smiled watching her. As cliché as it sounded, it really was like watching a kid in a candy store. She selected a bag of coffee, several teas and an assortment of chocolate. When she approached the register to check out, Alen had the good sense to turn away. He didn't want to know what this shopping bag was costing them. Their income consisted of Alen's military retirement benefits for the next two years until he was old enough to start drawing social security. But they still had the proceeds from selling their home, vehicles and all their household goods before leaving Corpus Christi. So, he wasn't really worried about the money. They also predicted this would be one of their most expensive destinations for the first year. They would be more frugal later, they reasoned. But he couldn't help but wonder what would happen if they couldn't leave London for some reason. They couldn't afford to live there permanently, and if something happened to Addison and Layne, what would become of Darcy and Lizzie? He already knew that Grace and Tommy weren't caring for the dogs because they had three dogs of their own. But he didn't want to bring that up to Joan, yet.

She pranced out of the department, swinging her pretty green bag and said, "Now, I'm ready to go find a meal. I'm starving. But I do want to take a photo or two of the outside before we go."

"From what I understand, you're in luck if we find a pub with a Sunday roast," Alen told her.

"Isn't it funny that we have roasts on Sunday in the States and they have them here too. It fascinates me how many things are the same in worlds far apart and how many things are different."

"It is fascinating, my love. Have I mentioned lately that this whole traveling the world as house sitters was a wonderful idea, and I'm glad we did it?"

"Nope, not lately, but I know. Look according to my phone, Tattersall's tavern isn't far and they have a Sunday roast. We can walk it," she told him.

"Okay, but I should warn you, an English Sunday roast isn't the same as a southern US pot roast."

"It's not? What is it?"

"I've heard it described as a feast like Thanksgiving. It might be a beef roast, or chicken, or lamb with vegetables and Yorkshire pudding."

"I've been dying to try Yorkshire pudding! It sounds delicious. Let's go. I don't really care what it is, I'm hungry!"

After their lunch, they returned home to spend the afternoon with the dogs. They also learned their way around the shop, familiarizing themselves with the inventory and prices. Finally, at 4pm they received an email from Addison. She sent a phone number for them too. Alen decided this discussion warranted a phone call, and he promptly called them.

"Hi, is everything okay there?" Addison asked when she answered the call.

"Yes, we're fine, Lizzie and Darcy are fine, and the house and shop are fine. Who isn't fine is a man by the name of River Read. Do you know him?"

"Yes, he owns a consignment shop on the other side of the river. We got an email from the City of London Police too, a DCI Sharp. He said they need to talk to us. Do you know what about?" Addison asked Alen.

"According to the newspaper this morning, he was murdered in his shop. Yesterday."

"Oh, no! That's terrible. But why do the police want to talk to us?"

"I don't really know. What I do know is it's better to head this off than to make them wait," Alen told her.

"Okay. We just woke up. Layne is in the shower. We're at my sister's house. This is her number. Her name is Sheila Davis if you need to call us. Let me talk to Layne and see how he wants to handle this," she said.

"Just let us know what you find out," Alen told her, and they ended the call.

Leveled in London

That night they walked down to The Ugly Shakespeare for dinner. They weren't really hungry after the Sunday roast they had at lunch time, so they waited until what would be their normal dinner time of 8 p.m. when the shop closed. The pub wasn't busy at all.

"Hi, new neighbors," Declan greeted them. "Did you come for the Sunday roast?"

Joan almost groaned. "I'm sorry to say, we had a Sunday roast at lunch while we were sightseeing, and now we aren't very hungry. Do you have something light?"

"How about if we whip you up a fine salad, then? How about a roasted vegetable winter salad?"

"That sounds delicious and perfect," Alen said.

"Just promise to come for my Sunday roast next weekend, deal?"

"You got it," Joan said as he retreated to the kitchen.

"I think I really like him," Joan said.

"Me too," Alen said.

SCARLETT MOSS

Chapter-Six

THE MONDAY MORNING ROUTINE WENT off without a hitch. Almost. Lizzie and Darcy had taken to sleeping in the bed with Alen and Joan. Joan was fairly certain that since the dogs weren't allowed on the furniture, they probably weren't allowed to sleep in the beds either. But both dogs had been adamant that they were sleeping in the bed with Alen and Joan. They tried repeatedly to get the otherwise well-trained dogs out the bed, but it wasn't happening. Alen even tried picking them up and physically setting them back in the floor. He picked up Darcy set him in the floor. Then he picked up Lizzie, and before he set her down, Darcy was back in the bed. The pet sitters finally decided to adopt 'grandparent' rules. Their parents would just have to deal with the retraining when they got home. Mr. Darcy slept between them and Elizabeth Bennett slept across the bottom of the bed. Though both Alen and Joan were up and showered and having coffee when the dog walker arrived precisely at 7 a.m., Lizzie and Darcy where still snoring in the bed. Alen had to wake them. They were both thankful that no police showed up. They assumed Addison and Layne contacted the police and the whole matter was put to bed.

Their surprise visitors at 8 a.m. were Grace and Tommy, the couple who probably knew Addison and Layne the best. They brought breakfast muffins and showed up for their ten to three shift two hours early. They wanted to visit with Joan and Alen. Since they were ready for the day, Joan and Alen secretly welcomed the possibility of learning more about the shop owners. It turned out that Grace and Tommy were partners in the business with Addison and Layne.

"How did you meet Addison and Layne? did you know them in the States?" Joan asked.

"No, we met them here. Expats tend to find one another. Even living in a country where you speak the language, the culture, history, traditions, even holidays are different than what we've known all our lives. Even if you fully integrate into the society and culture and have a stable of local friends, it's nice to have friends that you share those commonalities with," Grace answered.

"I was surprised how young you are when we met you. Addison told me you were a retired couple. I was expecting people older than us, not younger," Joan commented.

"That's probably why we made fast friends with Layne and Addison," Tommy said, "We had so much in common with them. Layne and I both had dot com start-ups after college. After we built them for about fifteen years, we sold them and retired."

"Oh! That explains a lot," Joan said, "I was wondering how this thrift shop would support two couples living in a city like London. I know it's not really my business, but it's human nature to wonder such things. I'm fascinated with how people, especially young people, can manage financially to pick up and chase their dreams."

"Most expats have a different story. There are nearly as many ways to manage living abroad as there are people doing it. We aren't all trust-fund babies, that's for sure. But this shop is really a hobby for us. It doesn't make a financial difference, but it gives us a purpose, a reason to get dressed every day and not sit at home in our shorts watching the telly," Tommy answered.

"You're picking up the lingo already, how long have you been here?" Alen asked, finally jumping into the conversation.

"We've been here seven years. The first two years we explored the city, like you two are doing now. We traveled to Scotland and Ireland, to France and Spain, and then we were getting bored. That's when we met Addison and Layne, became friends and agreed to go into this business," Grace answered.

"Did you hear about that other shop owner that was killed? Did you know him?" Alen asked.

"River Read, Upcycled Kingdom, yeah, we heard. It's terrible. And we knew of him, anyway. He approached Addison and Layne about merging the stores. They asked us what we thought, and all four of us agreed we didn't want to expand. Not to more stores or more partners. We have it pretty good right now. The shop isn't hard to manage, it's still fun, and we work well together. When it stops being fun, we'll quit. I think Read wanted our location as much as anything. London is really funny. North and south of the river for a long time were like two separate cities. There was a time when hackney drivers wouldn't cross the river. The north side is considered posher, more expensive, than the south side. Some people I suppose still feel that divide. East and West London have a similar divide. West is wealthy, east is poor. Read's shop is in South East London. We are considered South West at this location, but we are right next door to Richmond on Thames, arguably the lushest of neighborhoods in all of London. Merging with us would give him access to a clientele he can only dream of in his location," Grace explained.

"I see. But how many of those Richmond on Thames people actually shop in a thrift store? I would think he would have a longer customer list in a lower income part of town," Alen said.

"That's because you're looking at it from a United Statesian point of view. You are in the land of antiques. In Texas a thrift store is someplace people take unwanted stuff to feel better about themselves for not just throwing it away. Here, when people make design changes, they consign the sales to someone else who wants to make a change. It's not as much a social issue."

"Now it all makes sense. Thanks for sharing with us and explaining. And I see you're a woman after my own heart, making up words when there isn't one that fits for you." Joan said. Grace laughed.

"I started using United Statesian when I was in South America. In some countries there, they are bothered by the word American to refer to someone from the United States. They maintain American refers to continents, and people from North America, Central America, and South America are all Americans. So, yes, I made up the word from necessity. Where are you two off to this morning?" Grace asked.

"We're doing the free walking tour of London this morning. It's how we like to start in a new place, but we better be going if we're going to make it! We'll be back by three. Thanks for bringing breakfast and coming early. It's nice getting to know you," Joan said.

Tommy and Grace fixed fresh cups of tea in the big kitchen while Joan and Alen got their back packs and made the bed, now that the dogs were awake. When they came back downstairs, Grace was waiting for Joan.

"I love the frog table runner in the kitchen! It really perks up that space," she told Joan.

"Thank you. I love frogs and collect them, my co-workers had this made for me when we were leaving. It doesn't really fit in with Addison's clean contemporary design, but it makes it feel like our space while we're here."

"I think it's a perfect whimsical touch. You kids have fun. We'll see you when you get back. And listen, if you should run late, don't worry. We won't dock your pay," Grace teased.

"Thanks!" Joan said as they all laughed, and they left to try to make their tour meet up in time.

Once Joan and Alen were safely out the door, Tommy said, "They seem too good to be true, should we check their luggage? Look for extra passports? I'm sure it's easy to pass a background check if you steal an identity of some small-town schmuck who never did anything but go to work and home," Tommy said.

SCARLETT MOSS

Chapter Seven

THE TOUR TOOK THEM PREDICTABLY to see Buckingham Palace, the home of the Queen; St. James's Palace, the home of Prince Charles and where William and Harry grew up after Diana's death; Westminster Abbey, home of the royal coronations, weddings, and funerals; and the Palace of Westminster, home of Big Ben. In front of the Houses of Parliament, they learned about Guy Fawkes, who was famous from the 1800's for a planned attempt to blow up the Houses of Parliament. Fawkes became a Catholic at the age of sixteen and later in life resented all religious education in England being dictated by the Church of England. Worshiping as a Catholic in England at the time was very difficult. He was caught and sentenced to death for treason for his failed attempt, but every year in November is celebrated with a night of bonfires.

They heard tales of Winston Churchill outside of the Churchill War Rooms and learned about Nelson's Column on

Trafalgar Square. The statue was interestingly placed on a tall column to celebrate Admiral Nelson's victory at Trafalgar Square, where he ultimately died. The statue was almost 200 feet tall with the sandstone sculpture of the admiral on the top. Around the base were four panels in bas relief depicting scenes from the battle. The bas relief was formed from the metal of melted down guns captured from the French. And they strolled down the Horse Guards Parade where the Queen's birthday celebration begins and learned about the Household Calvary Museum. When Alen learned that inside the museum you could take your picture wearing the uniform of a cavalryman, he was surprisingly excited.

"Are we going to this museum? It is on your list, isn't it?" he asked Joan.

"Actually, it wasn't even on my radar. I don't know why it didn't show up on any of the sites I looked at online. But you are such a good sport following me around, I'll make sure to put it on there somewhere," she told him.

"Great, I can't wait! Where are we going for lunch? I'm famished," he asked.

"The Lamb & Flag is what's on my list, but if you see someplace you want to stop instead on the way, just tell me. This list is not set in stone, Honey. And you get to pick places too, you know. I just was looking for interesting things and found so darn many it filled up the calendar, but we can change anything you want."

"Okay, but you do a good job. So far, this house-sitting gig is turning out to be educational and fun. You're doing a great job. It doesn't feel like we waste a moment, and it certainly hasn't gotten boring yet."

"Remember when we were in Corpus Christi, after George's funeral and I said I kept seeing all the stuff on social media about live life? And I wondered what that even meant? I feel like we are living life now. This is so much better than going to work every day, home, cut the grass, clean the baseboards, grocery shopping, and cooking boring dinners...the same thing over and over."

"Routine. I think I'm going to start one of those hashtag campaigns. #RoutineIsDeadly," Alen said.

"I think you're on to something. You might even become an Instagram phenom," she replied.

"A what?" he asked with wrinkled eyebrows and a scratch of his head.

"Nothing, Honey. We're here, I love these dark paneled old wooden floored pubs," she commented as they made their way to a table.

While they waited for their warm artichoke, blood orange, and feta salad, the conversation turned to their morning visit with Grace and Tommy.

"I'm glad Grace and Tommy came by this morning. I know it's not really any of our business, but it helps me to not be suspicious of them to know where the money came from," Joan admitted.

"I agree. And knowing that Read was making a bid to merge with them helps me know why the cops want to question them. Except that Addison and Layne turning down his offer would make him more likely to kill them, not the other way around. So, I still wonder how they ended up at our door. I'm glad we haven't heard any more from them, though. I figure that means they are satisfied with whatever answers Addison and Layne gave them."

Their salads arrived and they dug in. Not only because they were hungry, but they needed to hurry to get to the shop in time for their shift. Which they did, just in time.

"It's been pretty quiet today. There isn't much that needs doing, so sit in the parlor area and prop up your feet until a customer comes in. Have a great evening. We'll see you tomorrow morning," Grace said as they left.

Grace was right, the store was very quiet. After an hour, there had not been a single customer come through. Joan decided to pop down to the Mug Shot and get them a cappuccino and an afternoon snack to tide them over until dinner.

"Hi, Joan, how's it going?" Summer, the café owner, asked.

"It's going good. I came down for cappuccinos. Here are our mugs," Joan answered.

"Can I tempt you with an afternoon treat? Today I have mince pie and cherry pudding with orange custard," she told Joan.

Joan groaned. "I don't think we walked enough today to work either of those off. But if you can make it to go, I'll take one of each," Joan requested.

"I'll have your order ready for takeaway in just a minute," Summer replied.

"I'm sorry, I don't know why I can't remember to say takeaway instead of to go," Joan apologized.

"No worries. If I was in another country, I'm sure I would butcher the language. Oh! Not saying that you're butchering the language. But see, there you go. I can't be trusted with conversation. Here you go, enjoy your afternoon."

Joan laughed and thanked her.

The store was empty of customers and Joan and Alen were upstairs in the kitchen enjoying their afternoon snack when they heard the bell jingle. Joan popped up out of her seat and called over the four-foot-tall glass wall, "I'll be right down."

The two men in suits looked up and she recognized them. She turned to Alen and said softly, "It's Sharp and Fox. I guess you better come down too."

Chapter Eight

"Hello, Inspectors," Alen said offering a hand for a shake. Neither of them took it. He dropped his hand and with less hospitality, more seriously asked, "How can we help you today? I assume you aren't interested in a new parlor chair."

"Did you ever hear from Mr. and Mrs. Cotton?" Sharp asked curtly.

"Yes, we did. We passed your message on to them. I assumed they called you yesterday," Alen answered.

"No. They did not. At this point, we wonder, is it possible you disposed of them too?" Fox asked.

"What? No, we talked to them. They're in the United States. In Arkansas, to be exact. They did sleep in yesterday after the long trip. It was about 4 p.m. yesterday when they called."

"Is there anyone who can verify that you are supposed to be here? In their house, in their business?"

"Yes," Joan answered. "Their business partners Grace and Tommy Bell. As well as the owners of The Tea's Knees, The Mug Shot Expresso Bar, and The Ugly Shakespeare pub. Addison and Layne introduced us to all of them before they left."

"This Bell couple, they're Americans too?" Sharp asked.

"We need to talk to them all," Fox said.

"I'll get my phone from upstairs. I have Grace and Tommy's number," Joan said.

"Thank you. We'll wait here with Mr. Arny."

Joan returned and asked, "Would you like me to call them and have them come back to the shop? They just left about an hour ago."

"Yes," Sharp answered. Both Sharp and Fox were walking around the shop, picking up items and looking at the bottoms of them. Joan thought it was odd that they were shopping at this time. They continued going over the shop, picking up all the small items and examining them.

"Are you looking for something in particular?" Alen asked.

"Yes," Fox answered, but didn't explain any further.

Tommy and Grace rushed through the door when they arrived.

"We are Grace and Tommy Bell; we are part owners of the shop. Joan said you need to speak with us. Is there a problem?"

"So, you are aware of the Arnys and, to the best of your knowledge, they are supposed to be here?" Sharp asked.

"Yes, of course, they're house sitting. Why?" Tommy asked.

"Just making sure. You know, a shop owner is dead, another is missing, a stranger is in their house," Sharp answered.

"Okay, yeah, that makes sense. It could be suspicious, I suppose," Grace answered.

"Have you heard from the Cottons since their supposed

Saturday afternoon departure?" Fox asked.

"Yes, I've had two emails from Addison."

"How can you be sure they are actually from Mrs. Cotton and not just from someone with access to her email account?" Fox asked looking pointedly at Joan.

"I don't have access to her email account," Joan blurted before Grace could answer. Alen walked up behind her and whispered shhh in her ear. She got the message not to talk.

"Well, she said she was in Arkansas at her sister's. She called her by name, Sheila, in case you need to know that, and she mentioned Sheila's dog Tink...short for Tinkerbell. I don't suppose a stranger would know those details," Grace was beginning to sound agitated.

"She gave me Sheila's phone number yesterday in case of emergency. Would you like to call her yourself?" Joan asked. Alen squeezed her hand. Silently imploring her to stop offering information.

"Yes, get me the number, we'll ring her ourselves," Sharp answered.

"We received a report that the deceased, Mr. River Read, confronted Addison Cotton with the information that some of the inventory here is stolen merchandise. That this led to an argument. As you might imagine, it could also be motive for the crime."

"This is a consignment shop. Every tag is coded with who brought the piece in to sell it. We don't buy or steal, for that matter, any inventory. Now, if someone brought us something that was stolen, we wouldn't necessarily know that. But if someone were to tell us that something was stolen, of course we would look into it. But the truth is, none of us had any disagreement with the late Mr. Read, may he rest in peace. He approached Addison and Layne and wanted to become partners," Tommy explained.

"That's your side of the story?" Fox asked.

"Is this some tactic to try to pin the murder on a foreigner? Don't you know how much money we sink into your economy here, bobby boy?" Tommy replied. Alen took a deep breath and covered his face with his hands. This was dissolving into a bad situation quickly. Joan stepped in.

"Inspectors, you've been scouring the merchandise here. I assume you are looking for markings. Did you find any?"

"Yes, we were looking for specific markings. No, we didn't find any. Is there any more inventory here?" Sharp answered.

Joan looked to Grace.

"We have a store room for when we have inventory that we haven't put out yet, but Addison made sure all that was done before she left. No new inventory has come in."

"Thank you for the information. We'll be in touch. Do any of you have travel plans?"

"No," they all answered.

"Good, stay in town. We'll be in contact. And if you hear from the Cottons, please tell them it's in everyone's best interest for them to contact us. We don't want to have to start extradition proceedings." Fox said then followed Sharp out of the door.

"Oh, my gosh, this is totally crazy!" Grace said on the release of a deep breath once the door closed behind the cops.

"Typical! Just typical, try to blame the foreign bloke," Tommy exploded.

"Let's all take another deep breath," Alen said. "They're just doing their job. A man is dead. Obviously, they are barking up the wrong tree, so we just need to wait it out. I'm sure they'll find the right killer."

"I think we should try to help them find the right path," Joan piped up. They all looked at her. While everyone else was feeling a nervous wreck, Joan had the glow of excitement. She was on the path of adventure.

"Oh, no, you don't! My beautiful bride. Do not get involved in this, do you hear me?" Alen said. Joan smiled a twinkling eye smile at him, one she knew from years of experience that he couldn't resist.

"Oh, brother," was his only reply.

"Joan, can you give me that phone number. I want to call Addison myself to see why they aren't responding," Grace asked.

"Sure, but I think it's around midnight there," Joan answered as she pulled up the saved number on her phone.

"I know perfectly well why they aren't responding," Tommy pointed out. "If I was out of the country and the cops wanted to talk to me, I would know they were trying to pin it on me, and I'd run far and fast too. They have enough money; they don't have to come back. They can go somewhere that doesn't have an extradition treaty," Tommy pointed out.

"Let's all calm down. How about we close up early and go down to the pub. Let's have a drink and some dinner. What do you say?" Alen suggested.

"That sounds like a great idea, Honey. I just want to run up, wash my face and use the lady's room. You all go on down and I'll meet you there," Joan said. Alen looked at her suspiciously.

"You're not planning to sneak off and interrogate someone, are you?"

"No, no. I'll be there in ten minutes tops. I need to feed Lizzie and Darcy too. Then I'll be down."

The three of them left to walk to the pub and Joan went upstairs. No one locked the store door or put up the closed sign.

SCARLETT MOSS

Chapter Nine

As Joan was coming down the stairs from the bedroom, she heard the bell jingle on the front door.

"I'm coming, hold your horses, I said ten minutes," she called down. And then she noticed the lady standing in the middle of the front show room. Holding a big box that looked quite heavy.

"I'm sorry, I thought you were my husband. How can I help you?"

"You're still open, right?" the lady asked. She appeared to be in her early to mid-sixties. She was wearing a simple long-sleeved black dress and sensible shoes.

"Um, Yes. Can I help you with that? It looks heavy," Joan asked.

"It is. May I just set it here?"

"Of course. What is it?"

"It's items I would like to consign. I usually take them to

Upcycled Kingdom, but when I went there today, it's closed with crime scene tape around the door. I called my son and he told me about poor Mr. Read. He looked up your address on the internet for me, so I've brought them to you. My name is Maisy. Maisy Cooper."

"I see. Yes, it's terrible about Mr. Read. I'm Joan. But I'm not the owner here. So, I'm not sure about taking your items today. Is there any way you could return tomorrow between ten and three? Grace will be here then and could help you," Joan explained.

Maisy took a deep breath and sighed. "I just don't know what to do. I literally don't have room for this box in my flat. I live in a tiny flat. My employer gives me these things that she doesn't want any more. I've told her for years I don't have a place for them, but she doesn't hear me. Or doesn't want to hear me. Therefore, when she sends me out the door, I go straight to the shop and drop them off for consignment. I'm not in a hurry for the money, I just don't have a place to take them. I paid for a hackney to bring them here, but need to take the underground home. I can't do that with this big heavy box. Can't you please take it from me now?" Maisy pleaded.

Joan felt for the woman. She looked tired. Joan imagined she worked hard, and probably long days. Coming in the morning might not be feasible even if the rest of the obstacles weren't there.

"I suppose that will be fine. Come on back to the office and let me get your contact information so they can get in touch with you, okay?"

"Thank you, ma'am. I really do appreciate it. Where are you from? I like your accent."

"I'm from the United States. Texas. I'm just house sitting here for a few weeks. Here, this is a customer card. If you wouldn't mind filling this out, I'll get the box and carry it back here."

"Thank you," Maisy said.

With her customer card filled out and a proper farewell,

Maisy left walking toward the underground. Joan called out to Lizzie and Darcy that she would be back shortly, locked the store door and walked to The Ugly Shakespeare.

She bumped into Grace and Tommy coming out of the pub door.

"Oh, are you leaving already? Was I that long?" Joan asked.

"No, we're heading home. Our cook prepared dinner for us already. We were to stop by the shop and tell you to hurry. Alen said he's starving," Grace said.

"I got detained by a customer. A lady brought a box of items to consign. It's in the office and I had her fill out a customer card. And don't mind Alen. He's always starving to death. He can be so dramatic," Joan laughed.

"He's charming," Grace said.

"He's downright sensible that man is," Tommy said. "Talked me right off the ledge of building my own personal conspiracy theory. Have an enjoyable evening, we'll see you tomorrow."

When Joan entered, she found Declan and Alen talking like old friends.

"Finally, Sweetheart, I was starving. What took you so long?"

"A customer came in. Did you order for us?"

"No, I waited on you. But Declan was just telling me his specialty is pie and mash. I think I'm going to try it."

"Pie for dinner? You naughty boy," Joan said smiling.

"No, it's not like your pie," Declan started to say.

Joan touched his arm and whispered, "I know, I'm just teasing my husband. What kind of pie are you serving tonight?"

"Norwegian haddock and prawn fish pie with sweet potato mash," Declan answered.

"That sounds delicious, make it two, please. And I'd like

some warm tea. Chamomile if you have it," she ordered.

"I'll have it out to you in two shakes of a lamb's tail."

"I ran into Grace and Tommy leaving. He said you talked him off a ledge."

"I did. But it's tough. He might or might not be wrong. Declan said Sharp and Fox came in to see if he knew us and if he knew that we were supposed to be here. Hopefully, we're off the radar now. But Addison, Layne, Grace, and Tommy may still have something to fear."

"I do hate this for our new friends. There must be some way we can help."

"Not me. I saw the sign up for the Burns' Night celebration. I told Declan I was learning to cook. Especially celebration dishes in each country we visit. He says he'll teach me. But first I'm going to learn about pies. Then we'll tackle the Burns' night celebration fare. So, I'm sorry, but I don't have time to try to chase down a murderer. It's not my job anymore."

"That's wonderful, Honey. When do your lessons start?" Joan asked.

"I told Declan I have to check with the tour director and my boss to see when I can get some time off, but maybe tomorrow. What's on the schedule?"

"Tomorrow was a crammed day with the London Dungeon, Leake Street Tunnel, The London Eye, George's Inn and then taking over the shop at three."

"Wow, that's quite a day!" Declan commented as he served their plates.

"The next day would work, though. We work the morning shift and have the Jack the Ripper tour at six."

"My lunch crowd is down around two. Come by then, we'll make some pies before you go," Declan told Alen.

"Perfect," Alen said.

"Do you want to come too, Mrs.? You're welcome..." Declan started.

"Oh, no, this is Alen's thing. I've done all the cooking I want to do in this lifetime. Thank you. I'm sure I can find something to do to entertain myself."

"Now, see, this is how it's supposed to be. Let the cops do their jobs. We'll do ours. And play. And live life. What's that saying? Not my circus, not my monkeys? That's my new motto. Call me apprentice pie chef. I don't want to be the sheriff anymore."

"I understand," Joan said and they ate their dinner in silence, each planning what was coming next.

SCARLETT MOSS

Chapter Ten

WITH A FULL DAY PLANNED to be pure fun in front of them, Alen and Joan awoke early. Lizzie and Darcy weren't as keen to wake up. While Joan tried to stroke Lizzie's head and speak sweetly to her that it was time to get out of bed, Lizzie would use her paw to try to swat Joan's hand away, causing Joan to laugh. The dog rolled over on her back and seemed torn between continuing the game or going back to sleep. Darcy had his own game going with Alen, who was trying to make the bed. No easy feat with the two large dogs on top of the sheets and quilt. Alen would tug on the quilt, Darcy would jump up as though he was going to lick Alen's face, Alen would jump back from the bed, and Darcy would lie back down like he was going to sleep again, but his eyes were cocked to the side, never leaving Alen. They played these games for fifteen minutes until Joan went to the bedroom door and asked, "Who wants a treat?". Then she jumped out of the way as the two huge balls of curly fur launched off the bed, raced through the doorway, and virtually slid all the way down the stairs to the kitchen. When Joan got there, they were both sitting like statues in front of the cabinet where the treats were kept, not even breathing hard.

While the dogs were gone for their walk, Joan checked her email. Last night after dinner, she emailed Addison again. There was still no reply. She tried to shake off the bad feeling she had about the lack of communication. She reminded herself that the reason for their trip home was a family wedding and she told herself they were just busy. As soon as the dogs returned, Joan fed them their breakfast, locked the door to the living quarters, and she and Alen left for their fun day.

Due to the early hour, they went to the Leake Street Tunnel first. As they walked along, Joan explained to Alen that in 2008, a famous anonymous street artist known as Banksy organized the Cans Festival...a play on words from the Cannes Festival in France. He invited street artists from around the world to transform an underground tunnel under the Waterloo Underground station. The tunnel had previously been used by taxis to line up in anticipation of picking up passengers from the Eurostar train. Suddenly the tunnel entrances were boarded up with signs that said the tunnel was closed for maintenance. On a holiday weekend Saturday morning in May, the tunnel opened to the public, with thousands in line to see the artwork from street and graffiti artists from around the world. The tunnel is still an attraction and street art is permitted there despite being illegal in London. Every single day new art appears painting over existing art. At most any given time while walking the 300 meters, almost 1,000 feet of tunnel plastered with art, one is likely to meet someone painting a new piece. No one can calculate how many layers of paint and how many different pieces of artwork are layered in the tunnel because it's been changing daily for almost twelve years. Sipping coffee from their go cups, walking through the tunnel holding hands, Alen and Joan walked down one side looking at the art, and returned up the other. There was even artwork on the arched tunnel ceiling. Then it was time to move on to their next destination, the London Dungeon. They wanted to be in line when the attraction opened to have time for the activities they planned for the day.

"I hope we have time to come back and see this again before we leave. I bet it's one of those things where you see something new each time, even if there wasn't actually new art each time. Thanks, Sweetheart, that was a cool thing to see," Alen said still holding a cup of coffee in one hand and Joan's hand in the other as they made their way to the London Dungeon.

"The London Dungeon isn't our usual kind of activity. It's sort of like an amusement park with rides and shows. But it's all about the dark and twisty side of London history. Kind of like a haunted house of terror," Joan explained.

"And this is supposed to be fun? I never liked haunted houses. You know that," Alen said surprised.

"Yeah, I don't think you'll be sticking your hands in gelatin or cold spaghetti described as brains in this one. It's more history. But the history of the bad guys."

"Well, I did say that my bucket list was to follow you anywhere. I just hope I don't suffer a heart attack and die of fright," Alen teased.

Joan bumped shoulders with him and said, "Oh, stop it!" as they entered the medieval lift that would creak and groan lowering them underground to more than 1,000 years back in time. Almost two hours later when they left the dungeon, the conversation shifted.

"Oh my gosh, that was so much fun! If they taught history like that in schools, imagine how much easier it would be to learn,"

Alen exclaimed.

"I'm thrilled you didn't suffer a heart attack and die, Honey," Joan said sarcastically. "What was your favorite part?" she asked him. They walked along the sidewalk, holding hands as they almost always did.

"That's a hard one. It was all great, but I suppose the ones that will stay with me the longest are the Guy Fawkes' Gunpowder Plot, The Plague Doctor, oh, Escape from the Great Fire. What a nincompoop that guy was. Sweeney Todd made me glad I shave my head as I'll likely never visit another barber shop. The Whitechapel Labyrinth was fun. I'm not surprised we aced that — cool under pressure as we are. The Escape from Newgate Prison reminded me of a great psychological thriller novel I read once. But my favorite?" He asked.

"Um, yeah. Your favorite. Is it the same as mine?"

"Probably! My favorite was Jackie the Ripper! I think they're on to something. Jack the Ripper was a woman!"

"Yep, that was my favorite too. Tomorrow night we go on the Jack the Ripper walking tour. It will be interesting to apply that theory as we go through it."

"Where are we headed next? I'm starving."

"On the schedule for today was lunch at The George and the London Eye," she answered.

"What's the London Eye?"

"The big observation wheel by the river. Over there...you can see it from here."

"Would it be possible to reschedule that? I'm all for some lunch. But I think my adrenaline level is so high I'm going to jump out of my skin. And if I'm honest, I know I'm supposed to go for a cooking lesson tomorrow, but if we eat and head back, and you think you can handle the shop without me, I could squeeze one in today.

Besides, that looks like a giant Ferris wheel and you hate Ferris wheels."

"That sounds great. I fully support your learning to cook, 'cause our next house sit might not have three restaurants in walking distance with free food. And I don't like Ferris wheels. I got stung repeatedly by a wasp while stuck on one with no way to escape. But this is called an observation wheel because the cars are glass enclosures. You aren't strapped in with no way to get away or swat at something, so I think I'll be okay. But yes, we can do that another day."

"I thought bees and wasps could only sting once," he said.

"I did too. It turns out bees can only sting once because the stinger stays in you, but the wasp's stinger stays attached to the wasp and it can sting over and over again. I have no clue what I did to make it so mad, but it was."

"Here's George's. Let's eat and we'll head back to the shop. I can even let Grace and Tommy go early."

They opted for a salad that would be fast calculating they would be eating pie and mash again for dinner, but this time it would be pies made by Alen. They opted for a special roasted squash and couscous salad topped with pumpkin seeds.

"Alen, I'm getting worried that Addison and Layne aren't communicating with us. I don't want to think the worst, but what if Tommy's right? What if they are spooked and don't come back?"

"That's really not our problem, Sweetheart."

"How can you say that? We can't just walk away from those sweet dogs? What would happen to them? We can't take them traveling with us, we don't have a home. We certainly can't afford to stay here. Grace and Tommy already have three dogs, and they said they don't get along with other dogs. Can you imagine what it would cost to fly them somewhere? Anywhere? I don't want to sound selfish. I really like Lizzy and Darcy. They are sweet and funny and really good dogs, but I'm not ready to give up traveling yet."

"We have three weeks for all of this to work out. If it doesn't, we'll figure out something. Try not to let it worry you. We won't abandon the dogs, I promise. But it will all be okay. At least now that the cops aren't thinking we're involved."

They took the underground back home, remembering to swipe their oyster cards on and swipe off. Walking back to the shop and house, Joan told Alen to go ahead to The Ugly Shakespeare. She wanted to foster the burgeoning friendship between Declan and Alen. And she wanted to talk to Grace.

Chapter Eleven

"You're back early!" Grace said when Joan entered through the front door of the shop, ringing the bell above the door. Lizzie and Darcy jumped up from their napping position in front of the glass wall in the kitchen overlooking the shop and each gave one soft bark, greeting Joan.

"Hello, Lizzie and Darcy. I'm home. But I'll be down here for a while, you can keep napping." They barked again.

"Oh, Alen went to the pub to learn to make a meat pie. He'll be home later," Joan explained to the dogs. That satisfied the dogs, who stretched, circled, and laid back down to continue their afternoon nap.

"Yeah, we had such a blast at the London Dungeon we decided to save the London Eye for another day. I really just want to take photos from there. Honestly, I can't decide if I want to do it in the daylight hours or the night time as far as photos go. I haven't taken nearly as many pictures from here as I did in Edinburgh," she explained.

"Well, there aren't as many men in kilts playing bagpipes here," Grace teased.

"I don't suppose I'll ever live that down. But you're right. City streets and buildings don't seem nearly as interesting as a kilted man. But we still have a lot to see before we go. How's it going this morning? If you want, I can take over and you guys can leave early."

"Actually, I wanted to talk to you. I sent Tommy to his weekly poker afternoon with friends to get him out of here. He is so worried about this murder. And Addison isn't answering my emails. Is she answering yours?" Grace asked.

"No. I'm worried about it too, but Alen doesn't seem to be. We could try to call her sister, Sheila. It's early morning there. Maybe we can catch her."

"I tried a few minutes ago. We may have another problem. Yesterday the inspectors were looking at all of the merchandise looking for markings to prove or disprove the allegation that we have stolen merchandise, right?"

"Yes, and they seemed to find nothing alarming. Declan said they did confirm with him that it was planned for us to be here. I think we're off the hook."

"Maybe. Maybe not. And you may be off the hook. But we aren't. I'm surprised they haven't already hauled us in for question once they found out we are co-owners of the shop. If someone with this shop is suspected because of a rift with Read, why are they only looking at Addison and Layne and not us too?" Grace wondered aloud.

"Hmm, that is an interesting observation," Joan agreed.

"And here is another observation. The items that woman brought in right after the cops left have markings on them. Like museum inventory markings. Coincidence?"

"You're kidding! She seemed like a tired sweet little old lady. Do you think she's trying to plant evidence?"

"I don't know. When I found it, I sent Tommy out and tried to call Addison. I know we should call the cops, but honestly, I'm terrified to get them involved. What if she was sent to plant the items as evidence to frame us. What exactly was her story again?"

"She said her employer, her word not mine, gives her boxes of items regularly that she doesn't want. But she has no room for them and she usually sells through Upcycled Kingdom, but she went there and the store was closed. She insisted on leaving them saying she had no room in her tiny flat to take the box home. A woeful tale of not having enough money to take a taxi home with the box and not being able to take it on the underground. I honestly felt sorry for her. I should go talk to her. Let's call her and see if I can talk to her before time for me to be here to work."

"Don't worry about that. Tommy won't be home until late tonight. These poker tournaments last forever. I'm staying here. But what about Alen?"

"Alen is cooking with Declan. If he comes by looking for me for some reason, just tell him —hmm, what to tell him? I don't want to lie to him. We never lie to one another. But if you tell him where I've gone and why, he'll lose his mind. Just tell him I've gone to talk to a lady about some merchandise for the shop for you. That's true, right?"

"Yep, that'll work. Here's Maisy's number."

Joan called Maisy. Maisy explained she was at work and couldn't accept a visitor but agreed to meet her for a spot of afternoon tea and gave her an address. "I'll be back as soon as I can," she told Grace.

As Maisy instructed Joan, Joan called her back when she

exited the underground. Maisy gave her instructions to walk to a cafe and told her she would meet her there. She asked if Joan preferred tea or coffee and she would order for them. She explained she couldn't stay long.

~***~

Joan entered the quaint cafe and saw the senior lady from the shop the day before sitting at a table waiting. Again, she was dressed in a plain black dress.

"Thank you for meeting with me," Joan said as she slid into the chair across from Maisy.

"My pleasure, though I am curious what brings you 'round," she said. "I ordered us a sweet condensed milk pudding to go with our tea, err, your coffee."

"Thank you, I'm still getting used to the term pudding being applied to what I call cake," Joan said smiling and taking a bite before she continued. "This morning, the owner of the shop went through your box of items you brought in yesterday. She was quite enamored by them. She's had an idea for a whole new vignette to design around them, but she doesn't have enough inventory to carry it out. She wondered if you might have more that you're willing to part with. She hoped maybe you could only handle the one box yesterday and there might be more."

"No, like I told you last evening, my employer gives me those items. I live in a tiny one room flat and don't even have room to take the box home with me. She gives me a boxful several times a year, but I never take any of it home."

"You said you normally sell them at Upcycled Kingdom. Do you think there might still be some items there that haven't sold yet?"

"Oh, yes, I know there are. Mr. Read gave me a detailed inventory every month when he paid me for what sold. I have that at home. But from what I understand, the store is still closed, so I don't know if I can get my items back. He had a partner. I don't know what will happen to the shop now. If it was to close, I would be happy to give you my items. But if the partner is keeping the store open, I would feel bad about taking my items away. You understand, right?"

"Yes, yes, that's very honorable of you. What about your employer? Do you think I could talk with her to see if she has anything else she's willing to part with?"

"Oh. No. Please don't do that. I'm just a housekeeper you see. My employer is Lady Klara Pearce. She's not the kind of woman you ask for things. And she never entertains uninvited guests. I certainly would be reprimanded for bringing a stranger into the home, which is why I met you here. And honestly, I must return. She'll be home from work soon and she mustn't find me away."

"She works?"

"It's what she calls it, anyway. She has a magical green thumb with the orchids you see. They took over her greenhouses through three expansions and now she has a flower shop selling the overpriced things and she calls it work. It's really just another space for her to grow the curmudgeonly plants. The woman is barely human to man or animal but dotes on those plants like a mum with a baby."

"Fascinating," Joan commented. "What's the name of her shop? My sister has always had a fascination with orchids and grows them too. I would love to see hers if I can find time while I'm here. There's so much to see and do in London."

"If you like orchids, you should go see them. Though they're pricey. Some of them sell for hundreds of pounds. But her shop is like a museum of plants. It's called Lady Orchid's Nursery. Like I said, a mum with her baby," Maisy said. She rose from her seat and started for the register.

"Please, let this be my treat. I appreciate you taking time from work to meet me. I hope we have the occasion to talk again while I'm in London."

"Thank you, Joan. It's been a pleasure meeting you. I hope the shop does well with my items. If I hear about what the other shop is doing and they are closing, I'll be sure and bring more your way."

"Thanks, Maisy," she answered. Once Maisy walked out of the store, Joan checked her watch and pulled out her phone. She Googled Lady Orchid's Nursery, found the address and it said the shop closed at 4 p.m. There was not enough time to get there before they closed. She would have to wait another day. She sat there finishing her pudding and coffee and wondered if Maisy's use of the word museum in reference to the woman's shop had any significance or if it was yet another coincidence. She really couldn't imagine Maisy being anything other than authentic. She didn't think she was trying to frame Love It or Thrift It. But for some reason, when she pictured a woman named Klara Pearce, Cruella de Vil came to mind.

Joan returned to the shop with information and new suspicions to talk to Grace about. But when she opened the door, activating the bell, she noticed a group of four women shopping together. They were spread out throughout the shop but carrying on a conversation with each other. Apparently, one of their daughters was moving out from under mummy and daddy's roof, and the women were looking for items to help furnish it. Joan thought, *what a difference a culture makes. A young woman in the United States would be appalled at her mother and her mother's friends selecting decor items for her first home. But here, it appeared to be a perfectly normal thing.*

Joan didn't complain when they finished cashing out the shoppers who collectively spent several hundreds of pounds on knickknacks. She did learn through the course of the conversation that the daughter in question was firm about picking out her own furniture, but the women had her blessing to select the other items as she didn't have time for all that with her new career.

Once they left, Grace said, "I sure wish we could use those new items Maisy brought in. But there's no way I'm going to display them now. What did you find out?"

"I really don't think she brought them in to set us up. She doesn't seem like that kind of woman. But she did call her boss's shop 'like a museum for plants'. I think it was just a coincidence, though. I want to go talk to the woman who is giving away boxes of stolen stuff to her household help. But Maisy said she won't accept unsolicited visitors at home and her shop closes at 4 p.m. Who closes a shop at 4 p.m.?" she asked theoretically.

"What kind of shop is it?"

"It's called Lady Orchid's Nursery. Have you heard of it? According to Maisy, the woman owns the store as a hobby. She grows rare or at least difficult orchids and sells them for exorbitant amounts of money."

"Yeah, I've been there. She doesn't really seem to be overly interested in selling them."

"From the way Maisy talked, the woman sounds horrid."

"She's not what you would call warm and fuzzy for sure."

"I'm thinking, Alen and I have the morning shift here tomorrow. Afterwards, he's going to work with Declan before we go on the Jack the Ripper tour. Maybe I'll have time to go check the place out myself and talk to the woman. Maybe I can find out where the merchandise is coming from."

"I'll come early. You'll have plenty of time. What time does Alen go to Declan's?"

"At two. After the lunch rush dies down."

"Are you keeping this a secret from him? I can come as early as noon, unless you don't want him to know what you're doing?"

"There's nothing to keep from him. We could leave him here and go together. I can't imagine he would be interested in going to check out the shop with the most expensive flowers in town. How about Tommy? Would he be interested?"

"Oh, no. I dragged him there with me before. He said he broke out in hives. They were invisible, though. But I'm sure by the time he finishes telling Alen about the event, it'll sound like he had the plague." They both laughed and went to work trying to rearrange and disguise all the holes left by the day's shoppers before closing time. Joan invited Grace to have dinner with them since Tommy wouldn't be home.

Chapter Twelve

For their first day working the shop's morning shift, Joan and Alen had a more leisurely start to the morning. After the new get-the-dogs-out-of-the-bed-routine, they went to the Mug Shot Expresso Bar. They decided dessert for breakfast wasn't such a bad thing. While they enjoyed the scones from The Tea's Knees, they were longing for cappuccinos this morning.

"Good morning, house sitters. I thought you forgot about me!" Summer, the owner, greeted them.

"No, we've just been much busier than we expected," Joan said.

"I figured. The bobbies came down and asked if I knew about you two. I assured them I did, but I figured they were hassling you. It's sad about that guy getting killed, but I know Addison and Layne wouldn't have anything to do with it. What can I get you this morning?"

Joan held up their two to-go mugs and wistfully said, "Cappuccinos, please. And what do you have that wouldn't be too sinful for breakfast?"

"Bubblin Nut & Fruit Wich is respectful or Old-Fashioned English Tea Loaf," she answered.

"Can you explain what they are?" Alen asked.

"Sure, the Bubblin Nut and Fruit Wich is an English muffin spread with peanut butter, sliced apples, raisins, and brown sugar and broiled until it bubbles. The English Tea Loaf is sort of a cross between what you call pound cake and fruit cake."

"I'll have the bubbling English muffin, please," Joan said.

"And I'll have the cake," Alen said.

"Coming right up," Summer answered. While she prepared their breakfast, she said, "Declan said you're learning to make some English fare from him, Alen. My kitchen is open to you too. I usually start my baking about 6 a.m. and I'd love the company if you're interested in desserts."

"Thanks! If my slave-driving wife frees up some time, I would like that."

"We can make it happen!" Joan said. She marveled that Alen really didn't get how excited she was about him learning to cook.

Back at the shop, Alen questioned Joan about her plans for the day.

"So, you and Grace are leaving Tommy and me here to run the shop while you two go off to some flower shop?"

"Tommy is an owner here. I'm sure he can handle it if you want to go along too," she said innocently.

"Well played, Mrs. Arny. Well played. You know I don't want to go to a flower shop. The question is, why do you? I'm beginning to wonder if I know my wife at all? First Harrod's and now this?"

"You knew me perfectly well in Corpus Christi. I worked. I kept house. I grocery shopped. I kept gas in the car."

"Who are you and where is my wife? The only time my wife remembered to put gas in the car was after it ran out on the side of the road!"

"Hmph, just checking to see if Alzheimer's was setting in yet. Anyway, now I have more time, so things I didn't have time for before seem interesting. Anyway, supposedly these flowers sell for hundreds of pounds. I just want to see what the fuss is about."

"Sounds like a good way to get out of work to me," he teased.

"You can come too," she reminded him.

"No, thanks, I think I'll stay here and try to sell this 18th century bust of some famous dude I don't know. And play with the dogs. That sounds much better. Tommy and I will do just fine!"

"Grace is driving, so we shouldn't be gone too long," she said.

~***~

Joan pushed on the dark green door with orchids painted on the center glass anticipating a bell ringing. But no bell rang, because the door didn't budge. She looked for a knob to turn or a handle to push and there was only a flat brass plate. Grace was parking the car and Joan feared the shop was closed. Then she noticed the sign with the arrow pointing to a door buzzer that said, "Please Ring Bell." *Hmph, I guess one can't be too careful selling gilded lilies*, she thought. And then she wondered where the phrase gilded lilies came from as Grace walked up to the door and pushed the bell.

A woman with perfect posture and a severe bun approached the door. She was tall and thin, and Joan thought of a ballerina. Her skin was wrinkled, though perfectly made up.

"Come in," she said as she opened the door. "Can I help you with something?"

"Actually, if you'll forgive our intrusion, I was in your shop a couple of years ago and found the flowers so magnificent. My friend here is visiting from America, and I wanted to share them with her, if we might," Grace said.

Lesson number one in investigating with a partner, Joan thought, *get your story straight first.*

Her plan had been to ask Klara where the stolen inventory came from, and now she had to figure out how to do that with Grace's new story. The woman surprisingly held out her hand.

"I'm Klara Pearce, proprietor," she said shaking hands with both women. "Welcome to my orchid nursery. Orchids are very difficult to grow and are fragile plants, so enjoy perusing through the plants, just please don't touch them."

"May I take some photos?" Joan asked.

"I would rather you not. Thank you," she said curtly.

Grace led the way, and Joan followed. They stopped at each plant and feigned appreciation for it. After walking around the complete shop with the distinct feeling of Klara Pearce's eyes boring holes into their backs, they approached the woman. Joan had used the time to steel her nerves against this cold woman.

"Did you say your name is Klara Pearce?" Joan asked.

"Yes."

"How uncanny."

"Why is that?" Klara asked.

"Do you know someone named Maisy Cooper?"

"Yes, she works for me. Why?"

"I'm currently house sitting for a lady who owns a consignment shop. A lady named Maisy Cooper brought in some items to consign earlier this week. They were magnificent and I asked her if she had more and where she got them. She said she didn't have anything else to consign and that they were given to her by her employer, Klara Pearce," Joan said.

"I see, yes, I give things to my staff that I don't want or need. What they do with them after that, I don't care about."

"I was just wondering if you might have other items that you're ready to part with. We want to plan a specific vignette around Maisy's items, err, I mean your items."

"No. I don't participate in such a thing. I don't mean to sound uppity, but my home is filled with museum quality art and artifacts. I have a niece who works at the Victoria and Albert Museum. She's a dear, but for every birthday, Christmas, and any other holiday, including our monthly dinner together, she gifts me those tacky replicas of museum artifacts sold in the gift shop there. They pile up. I give them away. She never seems to notice."

" Well, thank you. Your flowers are gorgeous. You certainly do seem to have a gift for growing them," Grace said and they both quickly left the shop, with Klara locking the door behind them.

Not knowing where the car was parked, Joan was following Grace. The further they got from the shop door, the closer to a run Grace got. She couldn't wait to get to the car. She was about to bust.

In the car, with the doors closed, Grace practically yelled, "I wasn't expecting that! I thought I was going to die when you just up and asked her about that stuff!"

"What? What did I do wrong? That's what we came to find out right? I did realize we should have gotten our story straight before we got there. But I needed to know. I think we found the culprit, though. Sort of."

"What do you mean sort of? You think she killed Read?"

"No, no. I mean the culprit of the stolen merchandise. Didn't you hear her. Her niece works at the Victoria and Albert Museum. A huge museum full of decorative arts. A museum would have markings on their items. Items the cops would know to look for.

This woman assumes the items her niece is giving her are gift shop replicas. But what if they aren't?"

"Oh, my gosh, you're right. Should we go to the police now?"

"I don't think so. I think we go to Alen now and see what he thinks. I tried to think of a way to ask the niece's name, but I couldn't figure one out on the fly. I'm not very good at this covert questioning stuff yet."

"Didn't you say Maisy called her Lady Klara Pearce?" Grace asked.

"Yes, she did. Why?"

"If she's called Lady, she's a member of the peerage. The family lines are well documented. We might can find it on the internet."

"Fabulous! Let's go back to the house and see what we can find. We have time to ask Alen what he thinks too, before he goes to his cooking lesson," Joan replied.

"Joan, can I ask you a personal question?"

"Sure. What is it?"

"Are those flamingos on your socks?"

"Yes, they are, but why are you looking at my socks? You're driving."

"I know. But flamingos. On socks. In London in January. It's hysterical."

"Happy socks make happy feet," Joan replied defensively, and then both women laughed.

Chapter Thirteen

"You did *what*?" Alen asked. "I said we weren't going to get involved."

"Well, I know. And I love you, but you're not the boss of me. And I didn't intend to involve you at all. I thought I could handle it. But now it looks like a museum theft. That's huge!" Joan said.

"As opposed to murder, Joan?"

"Oh, um. I see your point. So, you think we should tell the police?"

"Absolutely you should call the police. But just wait a bit. Let me think about it. I think much better when I'm cooking. We'll discuss it over dinner."

Joan and Grace looked at each other. It was a monumental mistake. The two women were biting their lips, tongues, whatever to keep from laughing at Alen's statement. Thankfully, Alen stormed out the shop door and turned left headed to the pub for his cooking lesson. The women erupted. Tommy sat silent and still as he had since they returned from the orchid shop. Every time one of the women would start to get the uncontrollable laughter to stop, they would look at each other and it would start again. Tommy finally couldn't stand it any longer.

"What in the name of Joseph is so darn funny? This is serious stuff!"

Joan sucked in a breath and in her best deep imitation of Alen's voice said, "I think better when I'm cooking." And both women released peals of laughter again.

"The man has cooked exactly three times in his life," Joan explained when Tommy still looked confused. Finally, the laughter died.

"I'll go get my laptop. We need to find out who Klara Pearce's niece is," Joan said.

"I'll go get us some coffee and lunch. I'll be right back," Grace said.

Alen returned at 4:30.

"I've been thinking about it," he said when he walked through the front door of the shop. Joan was standing there waiting for him. But she quickly put her index finger to her lips and her eyes darted to the interior of the shop where Grace was talking to a customer.

"Come on, we have to go or we'll be late. It's rush hour, the tube will be packed," Joan said grabbing Alen's hand to pull him out of the shop.

"Wait! I have to change clothes," he said. Joan looked at him, he was covered in flour. She laughed.

"Okay, go, hurry, I'll wait here. We can talk on the tube," she responded having picked up the local name for the underground train.

In their seats, heading toward Whitechapel, Joan, in an effort to sooth what she perceived to be a frustrated if not angry Alen, asked about his cooking class.

"What kind of pie did you make today?"

"We made Chicken, Leek, Caerphilly Cheese and Prune Pie," he answered.

"What an interesting combination," she mused. "Did you try it? Was it good?"

"No, it wasn't ready when I had to leave. I finally met Declan's wife. Her name is Connie. And in a very interesting twist, I discovered that she is the partner in the Upcycled Kingdom who found the dead River Read."

"You're joking, right?" she asked stunned.

"Not at all. And if that's not odd enough...he was her ex-husband."

"No way!"

"Yep. What did you two girl sleuths discover once I left? Because I know you well enough to know you didn't just drop it," he said affectionately. He apparently was over being miffed at her. He sounded almost proud now.

"We found that Lady Klara Pearce has a total of two nieces. One is in her early thirties, the other is sixteen. We are assuming the older is the employee of the V&A, and her name is Holly Hunt. I plan to go there tomorrow and talk with her," Joan said boldly, but quietly. No one seemed to talk on the Tube and it would have been too easy for someone to overhear her.

"I'll go with you," he said.

"I guess this means, while you were cooking and thinking and meeting someone else involved in this case, you decided it's not time to call the police yet?"

"That's true. I do wish we would hear from Addison and

Layne, though."

"Oh! I forgot to tell you. Addison called this afternoon. They weren't avoiding us. They went on a trip to the Ozark Mountains with her sister and an ice storm hit. All communication was down and they were stranded there. They just got back in the middle of the night our time. They plan to call the police this afternoon to see what's going on, and she'll email us. They aren't ready to get on a plane back as yet because the wedding they went back for isn't until this weekend. But they said after that, if they need to, they will come back. We are hoping to clear them before that. But we won't have to worry about Lizzie and Darcy, in any case. They will be coming back, she said."

"Well, there's one relief. Let's go see what these experts say about Jack the Ripper. And maybe you could tell me why I, a former sheriff, have goosebumps, right now?"

"Remember watching episodes of *Murder She Wrote* and thinking how silly it was that everywhere she went there was a dead body?" Joan asked.

"Yep. You know what they say. Truth is stranger than fiction."

Chapter Fourteen

"My lovely bride, how are we going to find this generous niece who gifts museum objets d'art?"

"Last night, I searched LinkedIn for employees of the Victoria and Albert Museum. There were over a thousand with accounts, but then I found there were just over 700 who live in London. So, I went through them all. I found Holly's account, and it listed that she worked in the Technical Services Department. I had no clue what that meant, but on the museum website, I learned that department is responsible for changing out the exhibits and artifacts. They install, pack, move, and mount the artifacts."

"Well, that seems like a good way for things to get lost or displaced. So, how do we find her?"

"I don't think we can just walk in and demand to speak to her, right?"

"No, I don't think that would go over too well, unless we find a costume shop and get you a bobby uniform."

"Don't be silly. On the museum website I learned where an exhibit has just closed and another is about to open. If we can find those places, we might find our girl working."

"You are not only a masterful social activities director, you're a whiz at research. Okay, so, do you think we can find her and get back here in time to work?"

"If we're lucky. But the museum is huge, with over two million objects. It's more than twice the space of Harrod's. So, it all depends on when we find her. But we don't have to worry about the shop. Grace and Tommy will take care of it as long as we are trying to solve this thing. And today is River Read's funeral. Addison wants us to close the shop out of respect for Connie and Declan. It turns out they are very good friends," Joan explained.

"Really? That begs the question then, if my memory serves me, didn't Inspectors Sharp and Fox say that Read's business partner said there was bad blood between him and the Cottons? Now we know that business partner was Declan's wife, Connie. And Addison says they are friends?"

"You know what they say, with friends like that..."

"Well, let's get going. It sounds like it might be a long day."

Joan put a sign up on the door that the shop was closed for a funeral and lowered the electric shades that covered the store windows like Addison showed her. They said goodbye to Lizzie and Darcy, donned their backpacks and headed out for the day.

"This place is really twice as big as Harrod's?" Alen asked, resigned to what he suspected was going to be a long boring day. But he should have known by now that no day spent with his wife would ever be boring.

"According to the internet it is, anyway, but I don't know what it will feel like. There are six floors and, according to the internet, it's 12.5 acres. I don't know if that is total floor space or the land size. I did locate the gallery with the exhibit that just closed. It's on level 2, which I think means the third floor. The new one that's opening in on level 0, which I think is the first floor. I have the room numbers. We might get lucky," Joan explained.

"Don't you think they'll likely have those rooms closed off to the public?" Alen wondered aloud.

"I'm sure they will. But we have a couple of options. We can either hang out on those floors and wait to see if anyone is coming and going from those rooms, or we can be bumbling American tourists and wander into the rooms. I think it depends on how closed off they are. Are there doors closed or just a rope across an opening?" Joan said.

"Hmm, I wonder if being bumbling tourist would land us back in touch with the local police. I really don't like that Fox character much, and I'm not sure about Sharp. He seems to be a little nicer than Fox, sharper even," Alen said.

"Oh no! You didn't just say that!"

"I did! Hahahaha. I'm hoping for ropes, because if we have to hang out waiting on people coming and going, it sounds like we'll be on two different floors, and I wanted to spend the day with you. And besides, if we bumped into her, how would we know?" Alen asked.

Joan pulled out her phone, punched a few buttons and Alen's phone dinged indicating he had a message. There was a photo attached of a professional looking woman in her late 30s to early 40s.

"Who is this?" he asked.

"That's Holly Hunt."

"How did you get her photo?"

"Off her LinkedIn profile."

"Cool. But Sweetheart?"

"Yes?"

"How do you know about LinkedIn?"

"Oh, it's a social media site where business professionals connect. Instead of posting about what you had for lunch and cute animal videos, it's about networking with business contacts and other professionals in your career field."

"Yeah, I know what it is. We used it all the time in investigations. I wondered how you thought to use it."

"Wild. I didn't realize that. Alen, Honey, I know all the social media sites. This planet is shrinking. It's a small..." Joan teased.

"Stop! Don't say it. That's all I need is for that earworm to occupy my headspace today. Here we are, let's go see if we can find our girl," Alen said.

On the first floor they quickly located the room where a new display was being set up. The gallery was cordoned off with a velvet rope between two brass stands. They could see the team working inside, and they unashamedly watched for a few moments until they were able to see each of the worker's faces. The workers were removing items from wooden crates, unwrapping them and constructing the displays. The team wore aprons that said V&A and gloves when handling many of the items. They looked at each other and shook their heads. Joan pulled out her phone and went to the galleries interactive map application she saved earlier to locate a lift or stairs to get to level 2. They found the same sort of activity in reverse. A team was in the process of dismantling, wrapping, and packing. After watching for a few moments, they realized Holly wasn't working in this room either.

"Now what?" Joan asked. She was just sure this was going to be easy enough after her research. But now she had no idea what to do to find the woman.

"Well, watching them work, it seems less likely she could just pick up something and walk out with it. How about that app, does it show where offices are?"

"No, I searched for them before. I even clicked on all the spaces outlined on the app looking for any offices. I only found a lunchroom. I'm not even sure if it's for guests, members, volunteers, or employees as it's near some classrooms."

"I suppose our only option is to just wander and see if we find her. At least there are some interesting things to see here."

He took her hand and they slowly began to methodically work their way through the exhibits. When they saw someone wearing a V&A emblazoned apron they would look to see if it was Holly. They spent the whole day there. Joan finally relaxed enough to take some photos. She was surprised that photos were allowed inside the museum. They were tired and hungry and were working their way back to the entrance to leave. Joan also felt like they had wasted a day. They had seen some lovely items, but that wasn't how either one of them would have chosen to spend the day.

Back at level 0 they saw her enter the first room they had visited that morning.

SCARLETT MOSS

Chapter Fifteen

THEY WATCHED. IT APPEARED SHE was a supervisor or something as she checked all the displays. Once she finished, she would thank the worker standing near the particular installation and they would leave. Presumably their work for the day was done once she completed scrutinizing it. When all the employees were gone and she was the only one left, she walked to the arched entrance to the gallery, turned and inspected the room as a whole. Joan and Alen were waiting for her when she unclipped the rope and let herself out of the gallery. Joan approached her.

"Excuse me. Are you Holly Hunt?" Joan asked. The woman looked startled.

"Yes. How can I help you?"

"I'm Joan and this is my husband Alen. I was wondering if we could have a word with you."

"I'm on duty right now. What about?"

"About your aunt. Lady Klara Pearce is your aunt, isn't she?"

"Yes, she is. Is she alright? Has something happened to her?" she asked frantically.

"No, I mean yes. Oh, I'm sorry. She's fine, nothing has happened to her."

"Are you reporters? What do you want?"

"No, we're not reporters. Is there someplace we can talk besides standing here in the corridor? Can we buy you a cup of tea in the cafe perhaps?"

"Fine, we can sit in the cafe over here. But I only have a moment. I haven't time for tea."

They walked to the cafe and sat a table in a corner.

"What is it that you need to speak to me so insistently about?"

"Actually, we've gone to a lot of trouble to track you down. You see, we're house sitters from America and currently we are sitting for a couple who own a consignment shop. A woman recently brought in some items that the owner fell absolutely in love with. So, we contacted her to see if she had more. She assured us she did not. It seems her employer gave them to her when she was redecorating."

"I truly fail to understand what this fascinating story has to do with me."

"Her employer is Lady Klara Pearce. We then went to your aunt to see if she had more items that she would be interested in consigning with us. She explained that the pieces we were so enamored of were gifts from you."

"Aunt Klara is giving away my gifts to her?" she asked, wounded.

"Oh, um, darn, I guess that was insensitive of me. I'm sorry. I was so focused on trying to find more items similar to them for a display, I didn't even think that it might be hurtful."

"Whatever. I buy her items from the gift shop here. Really, her house is so flaming full, I don't even know why I bother. But she's my favorite aunt and she paid for my education that landed me a job here."

"Oh, now see. That's so simple and I never even thought of that. To just go to the gift shop here. Please, let us treat you to tea. I feel really badly for bringing this up. I hope you won't be upset with her."

"Sure, okay. Tea would be nice. Thank you," she answered a bit calmer.

Alen asked what she would like and went to place an order for them all.

"Did she tell you how to find me here?" Holly asked, clearly perplexed and surprised.

"No, she didn't. I actually fancy myself a bit of an amateur sleuth. In all honesty, she didn't even tell me your name. I found you through internet research."

"I guess you are a Sherlock Holmes wannabe, aren't you?"

"I apologize again, I was trying to do something helpful for the store owner while she's away, and I guess I got carried away."

"It's not that big a deal. I get it. You'd be surprised how many Londoners haven't even been to the museum or to the shop to realize that, from time to time, they sell replicas of pieces on exhibit. Especially the special short-term exhibits. In my job, I take it all for granted, I suppose. I bet the items would sell well in a home decor setting."

"How long have you worked here?" Joan inquired.

"Almost twenty years. For fifteen years I worked with the Sculpture, Metalworks, Ceramics, and Glass department. Five years ago, I accepted a transfer to the technical department."

"I assume you studied art or art history, then?"

"I did. Yeah. I love the ceramics, especially from China, and the sculpture, and oh, I suppose it's silly, but I love all of it. Can I tell you a secret? Promise you won't tell my aunt."

"I promise," Joan said, flattered that the woman would confide in her.

"I love this place so much. You would think that I would get tired of it all and that I would want to go home to a flat with comfortable overstuffed chairs and mismatched quilts, and pillows. Possibly something over-the-top contemporary. But I found when I went home, I wanted more. So, I buy the items from the gift shop for myself, really. When it starts getting too cluttered, or when I need a gift for Aunt Klara, I take something older from my personal stash to her. I really shouldn't have been upset that she was giving away my cast offs. Do you think she knows?"

Alen brought a tray with three cups of tea and a plate with a selection of cookies, or what the British called biscuits.

"I don't think she suspects at all. I expect that maybe she needs to change things out from time to time like you do too. I'm excited to know that you get them at the gift shop. I'll have to check it out and see for myself."

"Don't expect them to have the same things you have. Their inventory turns over quite frequently."

"I'm sure it does. I will approach with fresh eyes to see what they have," Joan promised.

Holly looked at her watch.

"I had no idea it was so late. I'm sorry, I'm afraid you'll have to check out the shop another day. It's almost time for the museum to close and the gift shop closes early. You've just missed it. But you can also shop online. Thank you for the tea. I'm afraid I have to run. I have to close up the storage room and complete my paperwork for the day. It was nice to meet you, and I hope you enjoy your stay in London."

Alen and Joan both stood and shook her hand.

"She seemed nice enough," Alen said.

"That, she did. But Alen, do you think the items they sell in the gift shop, the replicas she called them, even have the museums tagging numbers on them?"

"No. No, I don't."

"We need to go to the store," Joan insisted.

"But it's closed. We'll have to come back."

"I know this store is closed. I mean our store. Or the shop, or whatever. We need to look again at those pieces Maisy brought in. I'll call Grace and see if they want to meet us there, and maybe join us for dinner."

When she hung up the phone, Joan told Alen, "Grace said she and Tommy are at the shop waiting for us. She said they have something to talk to us about."

SCARLETT MOSS

Chapter Sixteen

WHEN THEY RETURNED TO THE house, Joan and Alen discovered Tommy and Grace sitting on a sofa in the shop. They were each petting a goldendoodle. Lizzie and Darcy turned and looked at the door when the bell rang and hesitated a moment, trying to decide whether to leave the petting hands or to welcome the new hands. Apparently, they decided that Grace and Tommy leaving wasn't imminent and they greeted Joan and Alen.

"I didn't know they were allowed down here," Joan said.

"Yeah, after hours it's fine. They looked so sad when we got here. Even though they are usually upstairs, they can see us down here when we're working. It's not very often they spend a day home all alone. We didn't want to intrude on your space upstairs to sit with them, so we allowed them here. Have a seat, tell us about your day and we can tell you about ours," Grace said.

"We basically spent the whole day wandering the museum

looking for Holly. We finally found her. But by the time we got to talk to her and found out she bought the items in the museum gift shop, the shop was closed for the day. So, I suppose we have to go back."

"Hmm, maybe not," Grace said.

"Really? Why? What did you two do today?" Joan asked.

"We journeyed to the English countryside to attend River Read's funeral. It was an unusual affair, but quite lovely actually, don't you think, Tommy?" Grace said.

"Yeah. I never think about it much, but it wouldn't be a bad way to go," Tommy answered.

"We haven't been to an English funeral. Tell us about it while I make some coffee," Alen said.

"Apparently, they had the man cremated. But someone explained they used a water cremation process called alkaline hydrolysis. The result is the same, a bag of ashes, but the process doesn't use an incinerator," Grace explained.

"See, that sounds much better to me. I don't really care where I am after I go. But I hate being hot. The whole idea of being cooked bothers me," Tommy said.

"Yes, Love. But we aren't talking about you right now. Let me finish. Anyway, the funeral was at a place they call a stone barrow. It's like a man-made cave built of stone with a domed roof. They cover the building with earth and grass and it appears to be underground but it isn't. I imagine from a helicopter, though, it would look like a hill. Inside the walls are stone with niches to place the ashes and then later a cover is placed over the niche. His daughters arranged the whole thing, according to Declan. They are conscientious of the planet, I guess, and feel this is less harmful to the environment. Declan explained that while coffins in the U.S. are made of steel, the coffins here are made of chipboard or laminate with wood veneer. There is worry that formaldehyde used in the embalming process seeps out after the body decays and gets into the ground water," Grace explained.

"Fascinating," Alen called from the kitchen upstairs overlooking them.

"Disturbing," Joan countered.

"Anyway, Maisy was at the funeral. She introduced herself to us and asked if Joan was running the shop. I told her that you were trying to talk to Lady Klara's niece at the V&A. She said her son also works at the V&A. Get this...he manages the gift shop."

"Really? Hmm, how convenient," Alen said as he set down a tray with four mugs of coffee.

"Indeed. We can call her and maybe you can talk to him tonight and not have to traipse all the way back to the museum. We could even go with you and drive," Grace suggested.

Joan was already on her way to the shop desk and the file box with the customer cards to get Maisy's phone number. She punched the number into her phone and waited. She wrote down another phone number that Maisy gave her to reach her son, Greyson Cooper. Joan then called Greyson, and he said they could come to his house; he would be happy to talk with them.

In the car, Grace warned Tommy to let Joan do the talking and told him about her misstep at the orchid nursery.

~***~

After the two times talking to Maisy, Joan envisioned the poor housekeeper living in a tiny flat in an old building over a Chinese restaurant or something. After all, Joan hadn't been in many houses in England. None in fact except Addison and Layne's. She could only envision what she knew of from the U.S. and based on Maisy's claim that there was no room to take the artifacts home with her. She was surprised to see her son lived in a beautiful home. Not huge but decent sized, gorgeously decorated with a lovely garden out back. It was lit up with twinkle lights on the trees and ground lighting, so even though it was dark, it looked enchanting out the back windows. The inside looked almost like a museum itself. Much as she pictured Holly's house would after talking to the museum worker earlier in the day, or like Maisy described Klara's house. Alen was glad none of the houses they were asked to house sit so far looked like this. He was sure he would never be able to relax. Especially with dogs about. It felt like every place he turned, there was something fragile that looked expensive too.

Once all the introductions were made, Greyson offered them tea, and they declined. They got down to the purpose of their visit.

"How can I help you all today? You said you wanted to talk about inventory from the museum shop?"

"Yes. Someone brought in some items to our consignment shop earlier, and we became quite enamored with the style of them. We determined we would like to create a vignette around them but don't have enough for that. So, we started trying to track down where to get more. It seems the items have been passed around, but we found the source today. She's an employee of the museum, and she claims she originally purchased the items in the museum gift shop. We were going to take a look to see if there were more items we could use, but the shop was already closed. Quite honestly, your beautiful home is in the same style. Do you buy your items in the shop as well?" Joan asked.

"Sometimes. But not often. The items in the shop are expectedly pricey. I shop in the consignment stores as well. I suppose it's possible some of the items came from there too. I've only managed the shop for about a year. The objects in the shop are often replicas of the artifacts in the exhibits, and the inventory changes constantly. The items you see here, I also bought at consignment. I shopped at Upcycled Kingdom quite often. There is a woman that works there, I thought she owned the place until the death of the owner and he was a man. Anyway, her name is Connie, and when she would get things in that she thought I would like, she would ring me."

"Is there any chance you have a box or bag of things around you're waiting to replace? We really have our heart set on this particular display. And it sounds like buying items from the shop will be cost prohibitive," Joan asked.

"Actually, I just reorganized the bookcases in the library with a new stash of items I got from U.K. I could consign the items I replaced with you. Especially since I'm not sure of the fate of U.K. Wait here, I'll get them for you." Greyson said.

While he was away, Tommy and Alen sat in the chairs they were in and watched their wives. The women were swiftly but quietly and carefully picking up and turning over decorative items to look at the bottoms of them. They silently with no conversation each took one side of the room, working toward the back windows so that when Greyson returned, he found them staring out the window at his garden.

"Here you are," Greyson said holding out a famous dark green and gold Harrod's bag.

"Your garden is beautiful at night," Grace said as Joan reached for the bag he offered.

"Thank you. This time of year, it's prettiest at night with the lights. In the summer I prefer it in the daytime, though I don't get many daylight hours at home since I started working at the museum. Say, you never mentioned who the museum employee was. I don't know them all by any means, but if she buys that many items from the shop, I probably know of her at least," he said.

"Holly Hunt, do you know her?" Joan asked.

Greyson hesitated. The color appeared to seep out of his face before their eyes.

"Yes, I do. She comes in once or twice a month and purchases items. She's a strange one, though. She comes in when the new inventory goes out. Since she works in the technical department, she knows best when new exhibits are beginning. She'll come in during her lunch hour, browse a while, and then come back at the end of her shift and buy something. She doesn't seem to be impulsive at all. It's like she looks, then goes away and thinks, and then returns to buy. And she..." he stopped suddenly.

"What? She what?" Joan asked.

"Oh, nothing, I forgot what I was going to say. I actually like her. I never told her that my mom works for that old hag of an aunt of hers. I want to approach her as an equal without any of the old upstairs downstairs business."

"So, you're ashamed of your mother?" Grace asked incredulously, forgetting that she wasn't supposed to be asking questions.

"Oh, God, no. My mother has worked two jobs nearly all my life, since my dad died, to get me the education that I needed to do what I want to do, which is be surrounded by art and beautiful objects. She's the most hardworking, loving woman I know, and I adore her. I'm just not sure how Holly would feel about dating the son of a housekeeper. I would like for her to get to know me better before she makes that decision."

"Thank you, Greyson," Joan said. "Thank you for talking with us, for opening your lovely home to us, and for contributing to our new display. We're going to have to come up with a catchy name for it, maybe something using V&A or the museum collection. Have a great evening." Joan then extended her hand for a handshake. The men rose from their chairs, and they all told Greyson goodbye.

They didn't notice his friend out in the garden watching them leave through the window.

SCARLETT MOSS

Chapter Seventeen

IN THE CAR, ALEN SAID, "I'm starving. We missed lunch and our afternoon snack today. Let's go to the pub and have dinner."

"I don't think we should go to Declan's tonight," Grace said, "Let us treat you to dinner elsewhere. Then we can talk about this without worrying what might be overheard. Connie just keeps cropping up, doesn't she?"

Tommy drove them to the Savoy Hotel, and they entered the Savoy Grill. Joan had read about the lavish hotel and restaurant and had even perused the online menu. One look at the prices and she knew it wasn't someplace she and Alen were likely to go, even if they were the touted as having the best beef wellington in all of London.

"Do you mind if I order for us all?" Tommy asked.

"Certainly, go ahead," Alen answered.

Tommy waved off the menus as they were seated and

explained, "We don't need menus, thank you."

When the waiter came, Tommy ordered for them all.

"We'll start with the Waldorf salad on endive with pecans, beef wellington all around with sides of mashed potatoes and roasted field mushrooms in garlic butter. Your selection of red wine for us all, and for dessert, two portions of the warm chocolate torte with mascarpone and lavender ice cream."

"Very well, thank you," the waiter said.

"That sounds magnificent," Joan said. "Thank you for ordering for us."

"This is Tommy's favorite place. But we always order the same thing. I don't even want to try anything else as I can't imagine a better meal."

Over dinner, Joan and Grace told Tommy and Alen that many of the items in Greyson's house also had the presumed museum markings on the bottoms.

"The big question is, are Maisy and Greyson unknowing victims of having stolen items or do they know?" Alen asked.

"I can't wait to check the items he just gave us. If he knows they are stolen, he wouldn't just hand them to us like that, would he?" Joan asked.

"Yeah, and what did he start to tell us about Holly and then just stop?" Grace wondered aloud.

"I don't think he forgot what he was saying, do you?" Joan said.

"Nope. Not at all," Alen agreed.

"I have a plan," Joan announced.

"I had no doubt," Alen teased. And then they all listened intently.

When it came time for dessert, Joan moaned. "I see why you ordered two desserts to share. I don't think I eat another bite."

"I know you think that. I always do too, but you simply can't miss this dessert. It will fit, I promise," Grace answered.

"The million-dollar question is will I fit in my clothes tomorrow. But I do have to admit, it's by far the best meal I've eaten in my entire life, and totally worth it if I don't." Joan said.

"Thank you for bringing us, what a wonderful experience and like Joan said, if I should ever have the chance to order my last meal, that will be it. Then I know I'll spend eternity in heaven with those tastes on my tongue," Alen said.

"Honey, I love you. But good food makes you corny now that you're learning to cook," Joan teased.

They thanked Tommy and Grace again when they insisted that dinner was their treat. But Alen was quietly relieved when he saw the check was over £400.

When they got home, Alen and Joan sat down in the floor with their backs against the sofa. The dogs laid down on either side of them. Alen and Joan commenced with their evening brushing of the dogs and reflecting on their day.

"I can't believe I didn't think to take a single photo of the hotel, the restaurant or that truly beautiful meal," Joan lamented.

"I'm sorry, sweetheart. I should have thought of it and reminded you," Alen said.

"No, that's not your responsibility. I guess we'll just have to go back and do it all again before we leave," she suggested playfully.

"I don't think so. Do you have any idea how expensive that place is?" Alen asked.

"I do, actually. I googled the best beef wellington in London and I looked at their online menu. I know the beef wellington for two is £94 and doesn't include and salad or sides. I know the sides are £7 each. So, I hear you saying we won't be going back there to get photos, don't I?"

"Have you noticed. Several things we've done, we comment that we want to go back. Like the Leake Street Tunnel, The Savoy, and to return to see the inside of the Household Calvary Museum. How will we ever see it all? Especially if we keep doing things again.," Alen asked.

"I think this tells us that we should plan to come back to London again in the future. At least we'll know there is still plenty to do and see."

"That's a great idea. I think we'll be exhausted if we keep trying to see it all. But don't you have us pretty well scheduled for the whole year?"

"I didn't think you knew that!" she teased. "I do, but you know sometimes things happen. Trips get cancelled sometimes. We'll find our way back here sooner or later. I'm fairly confident that if Addison and Layne or Tommy and Grace ever need a house sitter, they'll call us first, don't you?" she asked.

"Assuming that Addison and Layne come back and the London police allow us to leave at all," Alen reminded her.

Chapter Eighteen

AFTER ARRIVING BACK AT THE shop and inspecting the new items contributed from Greyson, the couples discovered seven of the ten articles in the bag contained museum markings. Unless they were very bold, the four now considered Maisy, Klara, and Greyson off the hook as the murderer. It seemed they were innocent victims, just like the shop owners. But that left them only with Holly Hunt, the museum employee who Greyson confirmed bought items from the gift shop. That seemed like a fairly solid alibi. But the fact remained that somehow, Klara and Greyson both ended up with stolen artifacts and the only link between them, so far at least, was Holly.

Joan and Alen started their day with a different plan than was on Joan's schedule. Her plan had been a tour of Kensington Palace. When they devised their plan last night, they agreed that there were plenty of pictures of the palace on the internet and if something had to be dropped from the schedule, this was an acceptable deletion. So, they headed off to Declan's pub for a proper full English breakfast.

"Good morning, what are you two out and about so early for this day?" Declan asked when he greeted them.

"Grace and Tommy scolded us that we haven't experienced a full English breakfast and they said yours is one of the best in town," Joan said buttering him up the best she could.

"Man, do you live here? You're here from breakfast until closing time seven days a week?" Alen asked.

"I do live upstairs. But I have help. I tend to open up and close down, and the help works the busiest part of the day. I'm thankful for that, or I would have had to close yesterday for the funeral. I wondered why they planned it nearly an hour outside of town, but now I understand. It was a unique experience. Let me put your order in. I'll be back with your coffee." Declan answered.

When he came back, Alen asked, "I saw your sign for Burns' Night. Is that a big deal?"

"Oh yeah, especially for me. I'm a descendant of Robert Burns, the poet. Burns' Night is celebrated all throughout the U.K. on his birthday. There is a specially prepared meal, a ceremony that goes with. It's the biggest night of the year for us here. You'll be coming, won't you?"

"We would love to. So, there is a traditional meal? You know, I want to learn to cook a traditional meal for a holiday or festival each place we go. I've loved learning to make the pies, but would you teach me the menu for Burns' Night?"

"It would be my pleasure. But it's Haggis. I was going to start today; it takes a while to make it and I like to make it ahead."

"Actually, that's perfect. Our sightseeing plans were postponed for the day," Joan said trying to mask her excitement for how well her plan was unfolding.

"We'll start after your breakfast," Declan declared and went to the kitchen to get their full English breakfast, which included eggs, bacon, sausage, black pudding, baked beans, tomatoes and mushrooms. They were sure they wouldn't need to eat again for several days. Joan went back to the shop and left Alen with Declan. She hoped Alen would learn some information about Connie. No one could imagine why she would have pointed to Addison and Layne as suspects in Read's murder.

Joan and Grace worked at Love It or Thrift It while Tommy attended to some routine car maintenance and Alen learned to make haggis and hopefully some insight into the fate of Upcycled Kingdom from Declan.

Mrs. White arrived at exactly ten o'clock. She cleaned the shop first and then moved to the residence upstairs. She worked efficiently and quietly. Addison was right. She didn't care much for conversation, but Joan tried.

"Are you from London, Mrs. White?" Joan asked.

"Yes, ma'am," was her reply.

Grasping for something to talk about, she tried again.

"Do you have dogs? Lizzie and Darcy seem fond of you,"

"No, ma'am," was all she got. Joan tried the last thing she could think of, the one thing that most women couldn't not talk about.

"Do you have children?"

"Yes, ma'am," she answered.

Joan looked up from the front of the shop where she was standing to Grace in the kitchen above. Grace shrugged her shoulders, held out her hands, palms up, and mouthed... "It's normal."

Whenever the store didn't have customers, Grace and Joan

tried to figure out how so many pieces of museum property were floating around. Quietly, so as not to be overheard by the feather-duster-wielding Mrs. White. They mulled over questions like, wouldn't Greyson know about the markings? Wouldn't he notice them and be suspicious? And how could anyone steal items from a museum? They had in their possession sixteen pieces that appeared to be stolen from the museum. And they had seen no less than ten more in Greyson's living room alone.

Meanwhile, while learning the delicate process of making haggis, Alen asked about Connie and her store.

"Is Connie's store open today?" Alen asked Declan.

"Yeah, she's opening. I'm glad too. She's been one angry lass since it all went down. But I think the anger is helping her through the grief."

"Angry?" Alen inquired.

"Yeah, going through the papers after he died, she discovered he was planning to sell the shop. He never mentioned it to her, so she thinks he was going to cut her out of the deal. I got so tired of hearing about it, I tried to convince her that maybe he just had feelers out for a buyer to see if there was a market, and that, if there was, he would tell her then, but it didn't fly."

"So, she and Read got along even though they were divorced?"

"Not so much really. They worked different shifts. Mostly, Connie just worked when he needed off for some reason. The day before he died, she discovered items in the inventory she suspected were stolen. She confronted him about it. He swore he didn't know anything about it, but she watched him call the customer and ask her to come in because they suspected some items she was selling were stolen. He wanted to give her the benefit of the doubt as she was a regular customer. A little old lady housekeeper who sold items her employer gave her. Connie wanted to call the cops, but River insisted they talk to the lady first. Connie said, when he got off the phone, it was the woman's son he talked to who was also a valued customer and that they would come in later that day. Connie got mad and left. The next morning, she went by to find out what happened and instead found River's body."

"Wow. That's pretty tragic. Say, did you ever hear how he was killed?"

"Beaten. Cause of death was blunt force trauma. The murder weapon was an elaborate silver monstrance," Declan answered.

"A what?" Alen asked.

"According to Connie, it's used in the Catholic Church during communion or something. Anyway, it's tall and heavy. They don't know if, during the scuffle, it was knocked off a shelf and hit River in the head or if the killer actually used it like a baseball bat. The cops took it as evidence. Then they showed up asking Connie about it. The shop's inventory tag wasn't on it, and she had no idea who brought it into the shop. But according to the cops, they think it was stolen from a museum," Declan said.

"Really? How bizarre," Alen said.

With the haggis mixture ready for stuffing in the casing, they stopped chatting while they carefully stuffed the haggis and placed each one in a pot of hot water. Alen couldn't wait to get back to the shop to tell the ladies what he learned. But he had two more questions he wanted to get around to asking first.

With the haggis in the pot to cook, Declan poured them both a cup of coffee and then had a seat at a table.

"Do they have a motive for what happened to River? I mean was anything stolen from the shop?"

"No, that's the thing. They figure it was a disgruntled customer or someone else with a beef with the man. He wasn't especially nice. I mean, he was perfectly charming to his customers, but he had a temper. With employees, service people, what have you. He was very demanding and not tactful with people doing work for him," Declan explained.

"Will Connie keep the shop, now?" Alen asked.

"I hope not. We've talked about it. I think she's going to ask Addison if they want the inventory when they return. Now that she would get all the money from selling, it's more appealing to her, I think."

"If she's in a hurry, Grace and Tommy are here. You know they are owners in Love It or Thrift It too," Alen told him.

"No, I didn't know that, I wonder if she does. I'll ask her about it."

"Declan, thanks so much for teaching me to make the haggis. I can't wait until Burns' Night," Alen said preparing to leave.

"Yeah, we still have more food to make for it. So, are you telling me you're going to eat the haggis? Most Yanks won't get near it, especially once they know how it's made,"

"Joan and I ate haggis in Scotland recently. We liked it, deciding it tastes a little like meatloaf. So, you bet, we'll be partaking. We'll catch you later, probably for dinner. A good thick hamburger is beginning to sound good."

Alen rushed back to the shop to tell Grace and Joan what he had learned. Tommy had just returned from getting his car's oil changed and tires rotated too. Mrs. White was preparing to leave. Tommy offered to take her home.

"No, thank you. I'll see you next week," she answered him. And with that the quiet Mrs. White left.

Alen filled them in on this new information he learned from Declan.

"So, we aren't crazy that this stuff is stolen. I wonder how much stolen stuff is in their inventory," Grace asked.

Joan's cell phone rang and when she looked, she exclaimed, "It's Addison!"

SCARLETT MOSS

Chapter Nineteen

"Hi Addison, I'm putting you on speaker. Grace and Tommy are here with Alen and I. How is your trip?"

"The trip is going fine. How are things there? Is everything okay? No more visits from what Layne is calling the Sharp n Fox?"

"Everything is well, um...I don't really know how to answer that question."

They caught Addison up with all that was going on, and then she had some information to add to the mystery pot.

"We talked to the cops, and I think we're in the clear. They admitted to us that the murder weapon, some Catholic relic, was stolen from the V&A. And they also told us that Connie told them that River confronted us about stolen inventory. We couldn't figure out where that came from. Yes, River did contact us. But it was to see if we wanted to either merge businesses or buy his inventory outright. Neither of those made sense to us. Why would we buy his inventory when it was supposedly consignment merchandise? And we already have Grace and Tommy as partners and couldn't see any advantage to adding another. So, we turned him down. Layne talked to Declan and discovered that Connie found those email exchanges in which we clearly declined his offers. Declan said Connie felt that River was trying to sell out and cut her out of the deal. Maybe he was. We don't know, and I guess now no one ever will know what he was thinking. But we still couldn't figure out why Connie would fabricate a story about stolen inventory to point the cops at us."

"I might know the answer," Alen said. "I just spent the day with Declan. He told me that River discovered stolen stuff in his shop and that Connie was there when he called the customer to come in. But she doesn't know who the customer is. We're pretty sure we know who that was. But she wouldn't have killed River. She wasn't aware the items were stolen either. But maybe she was trying to get the cops out of her store to give her time to clear out any questionable items."

"Well, that could be. But I don't think so. I think my sister, Sheila, solved it," Addison said.

"Your sister in Arkansas?" Grace asked surprised.

"Yeah, so this wedding we're going to is for an old college friend. We had the yearbooks out flipping through them at a party the other night. And Sheila remembered this English student who had a crush on Layne. She was in Sheila's class, and she remembers this Connie chick saying that I stole Layne from her. It's not true. He never dated her or anything. They sometimes studied together at the library, but that was it. Anyway, I'd forgotten all about her because I didn't really know her all that well. We found her picture in the yearbook. It's that Connie. I always thought there was something familiar about her and couldn't place it. But maybe she's still holding a grudge, maybe she's still carrying a torch, or the torch is relit for

Layne."

"Oh my gosh. So, there's at least two reasons for her to point the cops in your direction. But it still doesn't tell us who the killer is. But it might give us a motive or three," Joan answered.

"Declan said he's trying to convince Connie to sell the inventory and give up the shop. But I'm betting if she's your college Connie, she won't want to sell to you," Alen said.

"Joan and I were just contemplating going over to Upcycled Kingdom to have a look around and see if we see anything that might also be from the museum," Grace said.

"Have you told the cops yet that we have stolen stuff or where it came from?" Addison asked.

"Not yet. We were hoping to track down the source. I hate to see any more innocent people caught up in this. And frankly, as long as you and Layne might have been considered suspects, we didn't want to give them any ammunition, so to speak. They are very suspicious, and the fact that we just had this stuff dropped on us after River's death might seem too coincidental to them."

"Good thought. But I have an idea. Go ahead and wander over to U.K. Have a look around. Drop the information that Layne and I aren't coming back and are sending papers to transfer ownership of the shop to Grace and Tommy."

"You're not coming back?" Grace exclaimed.

"Yes, yes, of course we are coming back. But if she can lie to the cops, what's a little white lie to see if she offers her stuff up to you. I still can't understand how she can sell the inventory if the items are consigned. She doesn't own them. Is she planning to steal it all, sell it, take the money and run? Or is she planning to pay the customers their fair percentage?" Addison questioned.

"I don't know. But it's getting late, and if we're going, Joan and I better leave now," Grace said.

"Call me back at Sheila's number when you get back! I'm dying to hear what happens," Addison begged.

"Okay, we will. Talk soon," Joan said and hung up.

Joan and Grace prepared to leave.

"Hold on," Alen said. "What are your plans? How are you going to handle this?" he asked Joan.

"I don't know. I'll figure it out on the way."

"I'm not so sure that's a great idea. You know, we never considered that maybe Connie is the killer. You could be walking into an extremely dangerous situation!"

"Hmm, you're right. I'll take care with how we approach things," she said trying to assure him.

"Nope. I don't like this at all," Tommy said, "Especially if Alen and I are stuck here with no car. But time is critical, it's getting late. We'll all go. Alen and I don't have to go in, but we'll be close if there is any trouble, instead of across town with no clue. Let's go," Tommy said, settling the matter. They didn't have time to argue. Joan and Grace couldn't think of any reason why it would be a bad thing for the men to be along.

They talked about different approaches on the way. As usual, Joan won out and would do things the way she thought was best. Alen had no objections.

~***~

"Hello, ladies. What brings you to the wrong side of town?" Connie asked when she looked up to see who was entering her store.

"Hi, Connie," Joan answered first. "We're shopping, actually. We thought we would have a look around to see if you have something we could use," Joan said.

"We?" Connie asked, clearly confused why Joan would be shopping.

Grace answered, "Actually, I guess I'm the one shopping. I

have an idea for a particular vignette I want to do at Love It. Usually we only use items on consignment, but I'm excited about this idea and don't have enough of what I need. So, I thought if I could find what I need, I could buy it personally and consign it to the store. I would have to find a good deal on it though."

"Addison is going to let you do a display without it being her idea?" Connie asked bitterly.

"Since Addison and Layne aren't coming back, Grace gets to do whatever she wants," Joan said.

"They aren't coming back? Are they running from the law? I heard the police wanted to question them," Connie said.

There were so many things Joan wanted to respond to that. But none of them would serve her purpose.

"From what I understand, they did talk to the police, and since the inspectors haven't been back to the shop, I gather they're satisfied. I'm so sorry for your loss, and I can imagine how antsy you are for them to find the killer. Does it worry you to be here by yourself with the killer still out there?" Joan asked trying to bring the conversation to a friendly caring tone, instead of the snarkiness Connie seemed to be feeling towards them. While she engaged Connie, Grace was looking around the shop.

"So, are you and Alen staying here? Are you buying their house and shop?" Connie asked. Curiosity was a magnificent motivator, Joan found. But she didn't miss that Connie skirted the question about being afraid in the shop.

"Oh, no, we have no desire to stay in one place, and we love being retired. We aren't bored yet!" Joan answered and laughed.

"So, what's going to happen to Love It or Thrift It?"

"Tommy and I are going to buy out Addison and Layne," Grace said, "We'll keep the shop. But we haven't figured out about the house. It's not really set up in such a way to sell it separately from the shop. We might have to move the shop so they can sell the house. Or maybe we could rent it, but it would have to be someone we trust to live there with the shop."

"Why don't you and Tommy move in there? I understand the appeal of having work and home in one place," Connie asked.

"We already have a house. We have three large dogs, and we have a yard. We don't really want to move. You have some really nice inventory here," Grace said.

"Are you finding what you need? Can I help you find something?" Connie asked.

"I haven't found just the right thing yet, but some possibilities. Do you mind if I keep looking?"

"No, of course not, make yourself at home. Let me know if I can help."

"Is it too soon to ask if you are looking for a new partner for your shop here?" Joan asked.

"I haven't decided for sure. Declan wants me to close up. Our daughters aren't interested in it at all. Say Grace, would you be interested in buying the inventory for your shop if I decide to sell? I could sell the inventory separately because we rent this space. I mean I rent this space."

"Hmm, I don't know. You do have nice items here. I would need to talk to Tommy first, but are the items not on consignment? How would we handle that with the owners?"

"I wasn't sure what I was going to do. But I felt bad for our customers. Most of them are regulars, you know. Some of them have been trading with us for years. River and I had business partner life insurance policies and his should pay out within the month. I decided the best thing I could do is pay our customers for their items. I don't have to feel bad about the hours the store has been closed, or if I'm just too grief stricken to open up or need to close early. Now

Leveled in London

I answer to no one but me and I own all the inventory," Connie explained.

"That was very kind of you," Joan exclaimed.

"Well, that would make selling it easier. Work up a price and I'll discuss it with Tommy. In the meantime, I'll take these two items now," Grace said, placing a vase and a carved wooden box on the counter.

When Grace and Joan left the store, the three women sounded like longtime friends saying goodbye. Connie closed and locked the door behind them and turned the sign to the 'closed' position. Grace and Joan hurried to the car parked around the block with their waiting husbands.

"You bought something. Does that mean you found museum items there too?" Tommy asked before Grace even closed her car door.

"I bought something to throw off suspicion. Yes, I found a few pieces with museum markings. I didn't buy *those*. We have enough stolen items! But she wants to sell us the inventory," Grace said.

"Does she, now? I bet she does," Tommy said sarcastically.

"What I don't understand is this...according to Declan, the murder weapon was a piece stolen from the museum. The cops looked at all the items in our shop, umm, I mean your shop, looking for museum markings. Why wouldn't they do the same at Connie's shop? Alen, does that make sense to you?"

"Two ideas come to mind," he answered, "Either Connie told the cops that item wasn't part of the store inventory, so they had no reason to suspect they would find more stolen items there, or the stolen pieces came in after the murder and investigation. I know the shop was closed for a couple of days."

"Why would someone lug a three-foot-tall silver religious

relic around as a murder weapon. And even if they did, why would they leave it behind?"

"I'm too hungry to figure that out," Alen responded. They all laughed.

"Let's get some dinner. But if we go to Declan's for dinner, we can't talk about any of this," Joan answered.

"I told him we would be there for dinner tonight, so I guess we better go. Tommy, Grace, will you join us?" Alen answered.

"I don't know, I think Tommy and I have to pour over our bank accounts to figure out if we can afford to buy two stores, and figure out what to do with Addison's house," Grace said playfully.

"What?" Tommy exclaimed. Joan and Grace just laughed.

"I'm beginning to wonder if we should add Connie to our dwindling list of suspects," Joan mused.

"She had motive and opportunity," Alen said.

Chapter Twenty

THE REST OF THE DRIVE to The Ugly Shakespeare was silent as everyone contemplated what to do next. Was it time to call Sharp and Fox back in?

All four of the friendly sleuths decided to dine on the evening Pie and Mash special featuring a Beef & Guinness pie with mashed potatoes. They couldn't talk about the case at all, because Declan was hovering with uncontained excitement about the preparations for the Burns' Night celebration.

He pulled up a chair and shared with them all the exact lineage that connected him with the 18th century bard. Just to toy with him, Tommy raised the question if they could attend because of the conflicts with Lightopia London and the Chinese New Year Celebration all happening the same week. Joan and Alen secretly hoped this case would be wrapped up so they would have the free time to juggle all the events they were excited to experience. But there was no way they would miss Burns' Night. Alen had helped prepare the haggis, after all. And he hoped to help prepare the rest of the festive meal.

After dinner, they all returned to the shop to call Addison back as they promised they would. After feeding Darcy and Lizzie, they gathered in the upstairs living room and Alen made a pot of coffee while Joan called Addison on speakerphone. Joan and Grace took turns telling her what happened with Connie at Upcycled Kingdom. Just as they were going to try to brainstorm together what they should do next, there was a loud rap on the door that led to the back alley. They all looked at each other, Joan checked her watch to see it was too early for the dog walkers. The collective pulse in the room rose and the energy crackled. Alen went to the door and asked, "Who is it?"

"Sharp and Fox," came the reply. Alen looked at everyone in the room. They no longer had to decide whether to call the cops. The cops were calling on them. Alen opened the door and invited them in.

"Come in Inspectors. We were just about to have a cup of coffee. Can I get you one or a cup of tea? Anything?" Alen offered.

"We aren't here on a social call. We need to know what happened when you visited with Greyson Cooper last night." Fox questioned.

Alen, Joan, Grace, and Tommy all looked at each other surprised. Joan remembered that Addison was still on the speakerphone.

"Addison, can we call you back? Inspectors Sharp and Fox are here, and it sounds like we need to talk with them."

"Go ahead and tell them everything you know," she said as Joan disconnected the call.

"We have to tell them all we know at this point or it's

considered obstruction of justice," Alen said to his wife and friends.

"Yes, Indeed. What do you know?" Fox asked in his normal snarky tone.

Again, they all looked at each other, trying to decide who was the best one to do the talking. They all looked at Alen.

"Monday evening after you were here, a lady came into the shop. She said she regularly dealt with River Read but his store was closed as she'd heard of his demise. She had some items she needed to consign. Joan told her the owners weren't here, but the woman insisted she couldn't take the box home on the tube and didn't have hackney fare to go home. The three of us had already gone to the pub for a pint and some dinner. So, Joan took the items and put them in the storage room. She told us about it at the pub. The next day, while Grace was working, she noticed the items had unique markings on them. And that's where it all began," Alen said.

"Where what began?" Fox asked.

"Do you still have the items?" Sharp asked.

"Yes, we have them. Shall I go get them?" Grace asked.

"Yes," Sharp answered. "Go on. I can't wait for you to get to the part about Greyson Cooper, since that's what we asked about."

"I apologize. It's a long road. The woman who brought the items in was Greyson's mother, Maisy. She seemed like a nice lady, and she told Joan her employer gave her the items and she didn't want them. We felt sure she didn't know that they might be stolen. So, Joan met with her to find out who her employer was."

"Who was it?" impatient Fox prodded.

"Lady Klara Pearce. Joan and Grace went to talk to her to see where she acquired the items. She said they were gifts from her niece. Joan and Grace researched the internet and discovered that she has a niece named Holly Hunt. Digging further, Joan discovered that Holly works at the Victoria and Albert museum."

Now Sharp and Fox looked at each other surprised. Grace came back carrying the box Maisy left with them at the beginning of the week. She handed it to Fox, who set it on a chair and pulled items out one by one inspecting the bottom of them. He nodded at Sharp.

"Continue. Where does Greyson come into this?"

"Joan and I spent the day at the museum trying to locate Holly to talk with her. We finally found her at the end of the day. When we asked her about the gifts to her aunt, she explained that she purchases items from the museum gift shop. But the shop was closed for the day and we couldn't ask anyone about it. We came home. Grace and Tommy were here, and they had run into Maisy that day at River Read's funeral. She mentioned that her son, Greyson, managed the gift shop at the V&A. So, when we told them what we found out that day, Joan and Grace decided to call Maisy to get Greyson's number, and they called him. He invited us to his house."

"Finally!" Fox exclaimed.

"We went to Greyson's. He confirmed that Holly did purchase items in the gift shop. His home looked like a small replica of the museum, so we asked him if he had anything that he would like to consign with us. He said he did and went to another room to collect a shopping bag of items. While he was away, Joan and Grace looked at all the trinkets. They discovered many of them contained the same markings, as did some of the items he gave us to sell in the shop."

"Are those items in this box as well? Or do I need to ask for them specifically?" Fox asked.

"We wouldn't commingle evidence!" Joan contributed before she caught herself. Grace had already stood and was on her way downstairs to the shop to collect the Harrod's shopping bag

Greyson gave them.

"We thanked him and left. That's all that happened at Greyson's. Why? What has he told you?"

"He hasn't told us anything. He's dead." Sharp replied. There was a collective gasp in the room from Alen, Tommy, Joan, and the returning Grace, who froze.

"What happened?" Alen asked.

"He was murdered. In his garden. Apparently last night. What time did you leave there?" Sharp asked.

Again, the four looked at each other.

"I didn't pay much attention, but I would guess around 7 p.m." Alen said.

"That sounds about right," Tommy added.

"Why haven't you called us before now?" Fox asked. "You obviously understand there are some serious crimes here and you just keep turning up in the middle of it all."

"We didn't want to turn people in who are innocent of any wrongdoing. To do so would have looked like we were grasping at straws and trying to deflect blame on others. That would have made us look more guilty, wouldn't it?" Alen answered.

"Maybe because you are!" Fox said harshly.

"No. We aren't. But we might know who is. If you would like me to continue, I would be happy to do so."

"By all means, go ahead," Sharp said, his tone kinder than Fox's.

"Grace and Joan went to see Connie Read Burns this evening at Upcycled Kingdom. Grace, do you want to take over from here?"

"No, Alen, you're doing a fine job, continue."

"Connie made an offer to sell her merchandise to Grace and Tommy. Grace asked her, wasn't her inventory on consignment too? She said, after River's death, she bought all of her customer's consigned items and now owns them. But in browsing the shop to purchase a few pieces, Grace noticed items with the same markings."

"Did you buy them? Do I now need to ask for those pieces so you can get them for us?" Fox asked.

"Of course not. we have more than enough stolen items in our possession. We left them there," Grace answered.

"Here's what I don't understand," Alen said, "Declan Burns told me that River was killed with an artifact that turned out to be stolen. I know you guys turned over every item in this store, so why didn't you find the marked items in Connie's store?"

The two inspectors looked at each other before Fox replied, "We don't answer questions about ongoing investigations."

"I didn't think you would," Alen said.

"We think Connie may have killed River," Joan blurted.

"Why do you think that?" Sharp asked.

"Because. I asked her if she was nervous being in the store alone with his killer still on the loose and she didn't answer me. She also tried to frame Addison and Layne because of her infatuation with Layne in college in the US many years ago and her imaginary perception that Addison stole him from her. And because she discovered that River was secretly talking to Addison and Layne about merging the businesses," Joan said.

"Also," Alen said, "Declan told me that Connie didn't know that River was trying to merge with this shop until after he died. He said she thinks he was trying to cut her out of the business and she's plenty mad about it. What if she did know that before he died. That would be motive."

"Oh my gosh!" Joan exclaimed. "When we asked Greyson where he got the items in his house, he said that a few he bought in the museum gift shop. But the others he bought from Upcycled

Kingdom. He said a woman from there named Connie would call him when she had inventory that he would be interested in. He thought she was the owner, until River Read's death and the publicity around it," Joan recalled.

"You know, Declan told me that Connie overheard River calling a customer and asking them to come in because he thought something they consigned might be stolen. That was supposedly the last time she saw him before he was murdered," Alen added.

"Okay people. Here's the thing. We now have two murders and a museum heist to solve. You all keep popping up in the middle and for the love of Pete, stay out of it. Let us do our job. Go do some sightseeing or something. Please!" Sharp pleaded.

"Yes, Inspector," Alen said. The rest of the room remained silent.

"May we at least go to Maisy and express our condolences?" Grace asked.

"Yes, that will be fine. Then I'm serious. Go about your business. And if you should learn anything else, call us and tell us right away. Don't make us come asking again." Sharp said. His tone sounded almost respectful under the exasperation.

"Yes, Inspector," they all said in unison.

Alen followed them to the door, "May I ask one more thing?"

"What is it?" Sharp asked.

"I'm really sorry to hear about Greyson. He seemed like a really nice man. Can I ask how he was killed?"

"Interestingly enough...with a garden tool from the museum gift shop."

"How do you know it was from there? Was it marked too?"

"Because it was a gift set. It was a William Kilburn fabric pattern on the set. At least that's what the box said. Fanciest garden tool I ever saw," Sharp answered.

"Thank you, Inspectors," Alen said.

"Go watch the changing of the guard, take a river cruise, something, but stay out of this investigation. I mean it." Sharp said, leaving.

I will, but I can't make any promises about my wife and her new BFF, Alen thought.

Chapter Twenty-One

THE FOLLOWING MORNING, AFTER THE dogs returned from their walk, Alen and Joan walked down to The Tea's Knees together. They decided to have scones and tea in the tea room instead of taking them home. Fern was busy behind the counter, but not as busy as she had been last Sunday morning. Joan was also feeling more optimistic. They decided to try two flavors and share them. Today's specials were pumpkin ginger with a sweet tahini glaze and glazed lemon crème. Joan decided to get a box to go to take to Maisy if she decided to let Grace and Joan come for a visit.

As soon as she returned home after breakfast, Grace called Maisy and asked if she and Joan could come pay their respects. The distraught woman agreed to see them and told them the name and cross streets of a cafe near her flat. She apologized it wasn't big enough to host visitors. They left Tommy and Alen in charge of the shop and took off to see Maisy. They both really liked the woman.

~***~

"Thank you for seeing us. We are so sorry to hear about Greyson. We wanted to pay our respects and assure you that we liked Greyson very much and we did not harm him. He was fine when we left him," Joan said.

"I never thought for a minute it was you. The police just asked me for anyone I knew of. I almost didn't tell them about you. I didn't want to get you into trouble. I'm sorry if it did cause you concern."

"It's fine. We haven't wanted to cause you trouble either. The items you brought into the store were stolen. We were sure you didn't steal them, but we've been trying to figure out who might have. We talked to Holly Hunt, and she said she bought the gifts for her aunt at the gift shop. We just wanted to check her story with Greyson was all. Then he gave us items to consign and some of those were also stolen. But he said he bought them from Upcycled Kingdom. We never even told him that they, along with several items we saw in his house, were also stolen."

"Stolen from where? I don't understand," Maisy said.

"From the Victoria and Albert Museum. There are quite a few stolen pieces floating around. We found some at the Upcycled Kingdom too. Unfortunately, when the police wanted to know last night why we went to visit Greyson, we had to tell them all that. And give them the items you brought us and the ones Greyson gave us. Luckily, we could also tell them that we didn't think you or Lady Klara Pearce had anything to do with it and that we didn't think you knew they were stolen."

"I see. No. I didn't know. I never even looked at that stuff. Lady Klara would give it to me, and I took it directly to the consignment store. But you said Greyson shopped there?"

"Yes, he told us that Connie would call him whenever she

got it items that he would like."

"Oh, my word. Do you think I was taking the stuff from Lady Klara and they were then selling it to my son?"

"Maybe, it's possible, I suppose. First, they have to find out who is stealing it. We thought Holly was a likely suspect. Especially when we found out she worked for the department responsible for unpacking and packing up the pieces for exhibits. But Greyson confirmed that Holly would come in a couple times a month to the shop and would buy the replicas the shop sells of items in the upcoming exhibits."

"May he rest in peace and I hate to speak ill of the dead and especially my son. I loved that boy so; he really was the apple of my eye. But he was so blinded by that cheeky girl. He has been since they were kids. She, of course, never noticed him but I think he has secretly carried a torch for her for many years. I'm not entirely sure you can believe what he might have told you about her. He might try to cover for her."

"Oh. Do you really think he would cover up a crime for her?"

"If he thought she would notice him for it. He's tried for years to get her to notice him. I think she's the reason he wanted to work at the museum in the first place. You know, I recall him telling me once that she came into the shop often. He fancied she hung out there to see him. He told me she came in often and would look at stuff a few times, then she would come back to buy later. He found it peculiar that she always selected pieces from the back, the last item on the shelf, never the one in the front. He said he thought she wanted to make sure it wasn't damaged from other people handling it. But you don't think she was stealing them, do you? That would break Lady Klara's heart. That girl has been like a daughter to her, since she has no children."

"I don't know. I guess that's up to the police to figure out now," Grace said. She noticed Joan seemed deep in thought, a million miles away.

"You know. There is no reason for her to steal anything. That family has almost as much money as the queen," Maisy said.

"Well, that's good to know," Grace said handing Maisy the small string tied box from The Tea's Knees. "Maybe it was a stranger somehow involved with all this. Thank you for letting us buy you a cup of tea and express our sorrow at your loss, I brought these scones for you from our favorite tea room. If there is anything that we can do for you, we would love to help."

"My biggest worry at the moment is how to pay for his funeral. I don't have a lot of savings you know. I would say, try to sell my stuff, but you said the police have it now and it's stolen anyway. So, there won't be any income from that," Maisy said sadly.

"Did you still have inventory at Upcycled Kingdom?" Joan asked, joining the conversation again.

"Yes, I do have quite a few things still there. But maybe those are stolen too. I don't suppose they will be able to sell them either," she reasoned.

"So, they didn't make you an offer to buy them from you?" Grace asked suspiciously.

"No. Why would they do that?"

"I don't know. I must have misunderstood something. Can we walk you home?"

"That would be nice. Thank you for coming to visit me. I don't have many friends, just a few people I work with. It's going to take a long time to sink in that my boy is gone. He was my whole world. His dad died when he was two years old, and it was just the two of us from that point on. It feels like I'm all alone now."

"I understand your grief. I lost a daughter five years ago," Grace said. "It will get a little better, but you'll always miss him. I

Leveled in London

hope you find some new purpose in your life to help fill the time that he did for you. We'll talk to you soon, again. I've enjoyed getting to know you!"

~***~

"Well, flaming scones. What are we supposed to do now with this new information? Most importantly Connie appears to be trying to sell you stolen – some of it twice stolen – merchandise that she said she paid the owners for, and apparently that's not true. And his own mother is telling us not to trust her dead son when he talks about Holly. Is it possible she's the thief? Do we call the cops back with our suspicions? What do you think, before the men weigh in?" Joan asked Grace.

"I think Tommy and I should open up dialog with Connie about buying her inventory. Maybe she was yanking our chain. Maybe she wouldn't actually go through with it. I hope not for Declan's sake. I really like him," Grace said.

"Yeah, I'm wondering what are the chances that we can catch Holly in the act? Greyson said she shopped once or twice a month. With as much stuff floating around out here with museum control numbers on them, I wonder if she isn't shopping more often than that. Let's see what Alen has to say about it."

They returned to the shop and it was busy. After all it was a Saturday. Talking would have to wait until later. Joan and Alen had already bought tickets for the Tales of the Plague walking tour. The tour started at 2 pm. Joan was considering not going.

"Don't be silly, I've got the store this afternoon. Tommy has a card game. You two go ahead. All this other stuff can wait until tomorrow. With any luck, maybe the cops will figure it out and we'll be off the hook," Grace reasoned with her. "I'll call Addison tonight and catch her up on everything."

"Thanks!" Joan said. "You really are the best. Getting to

know you might be the best part of being in London. Though we are growing very partial to meat pies." They both laughed.

Joan and Alen left. They had a busy two days of London experiences planned. In between it all, Joan planned to get his ideas about Holly and the museum ring of fire, as she now thought of it. It really was becoming an absurd game of regifting. She knew Holly wouldn't be back at work until Monday anyway. They might as well have some fun!

Chapter Twenty-Two

EVEN JOAN HAD TO ADMIT that getting away from the store and trying to forget about the case of the dead shop owner and the collection of museum artifacts floating around the city was a welcome relief.

Later she reflected that the Tales of the Plague tour probably wasn't the most uplifting activity they could have participated in, but it was educational for sure. They exited the Tower Hill tube station and looked for their tour guide. They found her standing next to a man with a rat on a stick. And thus, began the tour.

Alen and Joan followed the guide on their walk holding hands while they listened to tragic stories of London history. When the Black Plague struck London in 1348, half the population was wiped out. When it returned in 1665 to 1666 as many as 200,000 reportedly died from the plague. Most attribute the recurrence of the plague to the rapid and astounding population growth, a shortage of housing, and the vast amounts of garbage and waste littering the streets. This garbage fed black rats, which multiplied rapidly. Fleas carried the virus from the rats to humans through bites. When a human was bitten, the Yersinia pestis virus traveled through the bloodstream to the lymph nodes and created buboes or boils in the thighs, neck, groin, and armpits. Likely the scariest sight from the period were the plague doctors. They wore a suit consisting of a long robe, thick leather gloves, and a mask that resembled a bird's beak. The mask was also made of leather, except for the eyeholes that contained glass lenses. The beak of the mask had two small air holes and was filled with sweet aromatics like roses and carnations, herbs like mint, and sometimes vinegar-soaked sponges to help trap the virus and prevent the doctor from catching it. Many of the doctors used a long staff to touch the patients when necessary. By late 1666, estimates were that approximately 8,000 people a week were dying. Carts staffed by the municipality would travel through the streets calling out, "Bring out your dead." And the dead were buried in massive pits.

On September 2, 1666, a fire started in a bakery. And though it was devastating, many believe it may have helped end the plague by killing a majority of the infested rats and fleas. The Great Fire of London wasn't an easy cure though. Eighty-seven of London's 109 churches burned in the four-day fire. Ninety precent of the homes in London were burned. Residents fled to boats in the river or to the fields outside the city where many lived for months in tents and shacks following the fire. It took fifty years to rebuild the city. Officials quote that miraculously only six souls were lost to the fire. But scholars today feel that number is much larger. Possibly bodies in burned homes were considered victims of the plague and not the fire. Regardless, the city itself and the population suffered devastating losses during the years of 1665 and 1666.

Leveled in London

The tour ended at the Monument to the Great Fire of London. Ironically, if you believe the number of only six deaths from the fire, more people have died falling off the monument to the fire than died in the fire.

When the tour was over, Joan and Alen felt heavy. Heavy with grief and sadness for a city and its population. They had heard the story of how the Mayor was summoned from his bed the night the fire broke out and refused to give permission for the only firefighting measure they had at the time. To pull down and destroy the houses near the fire to deprive it of fuel. He reportedly went back home and back to bed.

They decided to take a stroll along the river to shake off the figurative soot to their mood. Instead, they envisioned boats full of people floating on the river, shrouded in smoke watching their city burn.

"You know, I thought when I discovered my friend the mayor was less than a moral character that I was the only one to ever feel that way. We've all heard the jokes and laments that all politicians are corrupt, evil, greedy, whatever. But I guess it's true all over the world," Alen said sadly.

"Yep. Power of any kind seems to turn many people into something new and not shiny like a new penny. Maybe it's the bad side we all supposedly have within us. I was thinking we should go out for dinner tonight. But I don't feel much like doing anything else. Why don't we head home, I could go for some dessert and coffee at Mug Shot's? Then maybe a salad later for dinner. What do you think?"

"I think as usual you have an awesome plan, my beautiful wife."

"You know what I like best of all about this house sit?" Joan asked.

"Yep. I do. You don't have to cook," Alen laughed.

"Correct! Let's go. The thought of coffee and dessert is already lifting my mood. I wonder what she'll have today."

~***~

When they entered the Mug Shot Expresso bar, as usual they were greeted by name by the owner, Summer Lane.

"How are my favorite neighborhood house sitters this afternoon?"

Joan laughed, "We are the only house sitters in the neighborhood this week, right?"

"Right. But even if you weren't, I think you would still be my favorites! If I ever decide to go on holiday, would you consider house and cafe sitting for me?" Summer asked.

"Only if Alen learns to do all the baking. I can make coffee... but I retired from cooking, except if it's the only way I eat," Joan answered.

"Give me some time and I might be ready," Alen said. "I found I do enjoy cooking. Especially special recipes. Speaking of which," Alen suddenly adopted a dramatic poor pitiful pouty expression, "we just came from the Tales of the Plague tour. We're distraught with grief for the city we've come to love and the devastation of the plague and fire. What might you have to drown our sorrows and lift our spirits today?" he lamented.

"Oh, my goodness. Well, you need the *Eternal Sunshine of the Spotless Mind* potion to erase the dirge. That would consist of a Mochaccino with an extra shot of chocolate guaranteed to raise serotonin levels, and a hefty slice the classic English banoffee pie," she offered playing into Alen's dramatics.

"And what exactly is banoffee pie?" Joan asked.

"Bananas, toffee or caramel, and loads of creme in a graham cracker crust," Summer explained.

"That sounds sinful, rich, perfect, and like the perfect recipe!" Joan said.

"Is that for here or takeaway?" Summer asked.

"We don't have our travel mugs today, and we would love to visit with you. So, it'll be for here. But can you make the mochaccinos doubles?"

"Absolutely. I think a double dose is called for here. I'll get them ready and join you at your favorite table by the window."

Joan took a bite of the pie, closed her eyes and savored the blend of flavors as well as the cold and creamy texture.

Before taking another bite, Joan said, "One of the things we discover as we travel is how many things are the same from one place to another. It's no wonder with the ease and amount of travel that happens in today's society. So, one begs to question, how in the world has this pie not become a thing in every corner of the world? Why have I not discovered it in over fifty years of life on this planet?"

Alen just nodded agreement since his mouth was full. Summer laughed and sat down with them. Joan took another bite and then asked Summer a question to keep up the conversation while she continued to indulge in the pie. Which she also noticed was lifting the heavy mood from the tour, just as Summer prescribed it would.

"Anything going on interesting in the neighborhood?" Joan asked.

"Of course! You know we all like a bit of gossip, but for now, the American house sitters are the raging news. It's going around that the bobbies are frequenting the quaint little thrift shop like drunkards at a knocking house," Summer said with a twinkle in her eye.

"A knocking house?" Alen asked.

"You know. A cat house. A brothel."

"Oh, for crying out loud. I guess I shouldn't have asked. Of course, in any country, the cops showing up every few days at where the foreigners are would be the talk of the neighborhood," Joan answered.

"I'm just having a laugh. Most all anyone is talking about these days is Harry and Meghan. But seriously, words getting around that Addison and Layne aren't coming back. I hope that's local tongue wagging because I really like them."

"Hmm, I wonder how that word got out?" Alen said, furthering the idea that it might be true to Summer's thinking.

"So, it's true?" Summer asked.

Alen and Joan looked at each other. "My guess is it came from Declan through Connie," Joan said.

"I bet you're right," Alen said, both of them ignoring Summer's question. But could they trust Summer with the truth? Or would it spread back to the pub as quickly as the rumor had spread down the street?

"Honestly, we don't really know how to answer that yet," Joan said, neither confirming nor denying the rumor.

Their pie was consumed, the mochaccino mugs were dry, and Alen commented, "I suppose it's time to go home. Maybe we can find something entertaining to watch on TV tonight."

"I know what you should do!" Summer exclaimed.

"What's that?" Joan asked.

Summer went behind her counter and brought back a large magazine. When she opened it up, Joan saw it was called *Time Out*.

"There's a musical in town at the Savoy Theatre. It's called *9 to 5* and it's hysterical. Actually, I think I remember it's based on a movie from America."

"Seriously? The Dolly Parton movie? That's an old one from

the 80s. And it's showing here?"

"No, it's a live musical, not a movie, but yeah, based on that movie. David Hasselhoff stars in it. It's bound to lift your mood. And the cops won't find you there," she teased. "Here's the listing. It starts at 7:30 p.m. tonight. We can check online to make sure there are still tickets available. I'll go check, be right back," Summer said, handing the magazine to Alen and going to her office and computer.

Joan looked at Alen and raised her eyebrow, questioning if he was interested.

"I'm not usually one for a musical. But it sounds like it will be light and funny. I'm game if you want to go. And if you don't want to, I'm perfectly happy curling up with you, Lizzie, and Darcy for the evening."

"I think we should do it! If there are still seats available..."Joan said.

"There are still seats available. But I booked you tickets, my treat. You just need to get there in time to pick them up at the box office. Here is the booking reference number." Summer said.

"Thank you! How sweet, you didn't have to do that," Joan said.

"I know. I wanted to. Now run along, freshen up, and enjoy the show!"

~***~

After the show Alen said, "That was really different from the movie. But you know, I loved it."

"I did too! I hope the show we are going to see tomorrow night is as good. It's a quirky live performance at Kensington Palace called *United Queendom*. It's set in the 18th century and is about the king's birthday."

"You know, when Summer handed me the *Time Out* paper, I noticed they have done the same type event with *Pretty Woman* as they did with *9 to 5*. I bet that would be interesting," Alen said.

"Are you saying you don't want to go to *United Queendom*?"

"It does sound a little stuffy, but it's up to you," Alen deferred.

"I say we go to the one we already have tickets for, and then if we want, we can go to *Pretty Woman* another night. We have already seen the movie. I would rather do something new. But Summer was right, this one tonight did raise my spirits considerably."

"Mine too!" Alen said as they descended the long escalator to the tube and their journey home.

"Shall we drop into The Ugly Shakespeare for a night cap before we go home?" Alen asked as they exited the tube station near the house.

"Sure. Maybe we can catch someone talking about us." They both laughed.

Chapter Twenty-Three

Sunday morning and the shop was closed for the day. While Lizzie and Darcy were gone for their morning walk, Alen and Joan walked down to The Tea's Knees and purchased scones for breakfast like they did most mornings. Today's selections were lavender and cranberry cherry. They couldn't decide which they wanted so they bought one of each and planned to halve and share them. They were excited about today's outing to Madame Tussaud's famous wax museum.

Joan made sure her extra camera batteries were charged as she prepared to get some fun pictures of the two of them with some celebrities at the museum.

There were many fun moments at Madame Tussaud's between Alen and Joan. When they visited the Royals area, they noticed that Meghan and Harry's figures were moved out away from the rest of the family.

"Wow, I suppose the Brits are offended at Harry and Meghan withdrawing from Royal service," Joan said.

"Well, if you ask me, the Queen is missing something," Alen replied.

"Yeah, what's that?" Joan asked quizzically.

"Her suit should have a frog broach, like yours. Maybe she wouldn't seem so stuffy," Alen teased.

"Do you think the queen looks stuffy? I've always thought she was a beautiful woman. And she must be a good woman, because she has dogs. I read she's had thirty corgis, though they've all died now. But she actually walked them herself. I also read that if she came into the room in her crown the dogs laid down, but if she was wearing a scarf, they got excited knowing it was time for a walk. A woman who walks her own dogs can't be too stuffy," Joan said.

"Right again, my love. Some days I wonder if there is anything you don't know at least something about."

When they toured the fashion section, Alen teased her, "Sweetheart, have you noticed, not a single one of these figures have on funky socks?"

"Apparently that's not a trend that's caught on here yet. Grace teased me about them too. But you can tease me all you want. They make me happy," she said defensively.

When Alen took her picture with the figure of Dame Helen Mirren, Joan was showing the actress her brightly colored socks adorned with happy garden gnomes that said "Gnomies are my homies" around the top cuff. Throughout the tour of the museum they took pictures of each other with some of their favorite celebrities. Joan sang with David Hasselhoff, whispered in Denzel Washington's ear, pretended to take notes from Ernest Hemingway, ran her fingers through Bon Jovi's hair, laughed at Robin Williams' joke, and tried to convince Pablo Picasso that his striped shirt didn't go with his plaid pants.

Joan laughed while capturing Alen's antics while he posed looking sternly into the open cell door of Al Capone's cell while Al played the banjo, pointed out the time to Anthony Hopkins as Hannibal, pretended to cover Bruce Willis' six, showed off a karate kick for Jackie Chan, proposed to Sandra Bullock, and frisked a leather clad Olivia Newton John with a big smile on his face.

They enjoyed the Sherlock Holmes exhibit, and Joan was sad she wasn't allowed to take pictures there or on the Spirit of London ride. The ride had them ensconced in a typical black London style taxi and transported them through the history of the city.

"You know, if we taught history that way in schools, I bet we would all remember more of it. It's so much more interesting when it feels like you're there," Joan said.

"I'm hungry," Alen said.

"Of course, you are," Joan laughed.

They found a restaurant nearby and ducked in for a light lunch. Their January watching the waistline salad for the day was a warm lemon and rosemary chicken salad with a shallot and caper dressing.

"That was fun!" Alen said.

"It was. Now, I'm thinking about trying to catch a museum thief. I think I need a disguise," Joan said pulling out her phone as Alen finished his after-lunch coffee.

"Where did that come from?"

"Seeing the celebrities in the wax museum. Holly knows me. If she sees me lurking around the museum, she might alter her plans. I need a costume. A disguise," she answered.

"As if walking around a museum in a Halloween costume wouldn't be conspicuous at all. You should just keep your head down," he countered.

"Like my red hair doesn't show up from across a room. Not a Halloween costume, which, by the way, according to the Party Super Store are called fancy clothes here. A disguise. We have time and they're open. We should go look."

"Whatever your heart desires. I told you when we decided to embark on this adventure that my bucket list was following you wherever you lead."

"I don't think that's exactly what you said, but I promise the party store isn't as big as Harrod's."

~***~

"I need to find a wig to cover up my red hair," she told Alen as they walked down the aisles.

"These Rastafarian dreadlocks should work," Alen said.

"I don't have a thing to wear with that," Joan countered walking down the aisle.

"Look, here's a Cher wig, and it's on sale," Joan showed him.

"Okay, yeah, that would work,"

"Oh! Wait, look, this black and silver one reminds me of Jazz Black. It's on sale too. This is the one I want." Jazz Black was a pub singer they met at their last house-sitting job in Edinburgh.

"Okay, let's go!" Alen said.

"No, I'm not finished yet. I think I should have some glasses."

"Why not just wear your sun glasses? That works well enough for celebrities walking through airports," Alen said.

"Really? And have you actually ever seen someone wearing sunglasses in an airport?"

"Actually, yes, I have," he answered.

"So, it caught your attention, and what did you think about it?" she asked him.

"Well, I wondered who it was. It was Cameron Dias," he

answered smartly.

"How do you know that?"

"Because it looked just like Cameron Dias wearing sunglasses," he said indignantly.

"In other words, the sunglasses did not disguise her but did catch your attention," Joan explained patiently.

"I see your point," he agreed.

"Furthermore, sunglasses would hamper my view, I think. Here, these glasses should work just fine. What do you think?" she asked putting on the glasses.

"You suddenly look like a librarian," he answered.

"Perfect," she said.

"Oh, look, here's a Sherlock Holmes kit. I could get that. I wouldn't use the pipe of course, but I sure do like the hat," she said excitedly.

"I very much think that goes the way of the sunglasses. It would call more attention to you. Then again, the black and silver hair won't exactly blend in as it is," Alen pointed out.

"It's okay. I'm not trying to hide; I just don't want Holly to recognize me is all. This will do, I think. I'm ready to pay and move on. Do you want to have dinner before the show or after?" she asked.

"After. Declan's special is hand-raised pork pie tonight. He promised to save us some for after the show."

"Great! That means we can either take a walk and stop in for a late afternoon snack before the show, or we can go home for a while and maybe get another piece of banoffee pie from the Mug Shot," Joan suggested.

"I like the idea of going home and spending the afternoon with the dogs. Maybe we will take them for an extra walk, and then try to get that banoffee pie. I definitely need to learn to make that!"

"You are my kind of man, Mr. Arny!"

~***~

Following a long romp with Lizzie and Darcy in the nearby Diamond Jubilee Gardens, Alen and Joan popped into the Mug Shot. This time they had to-go cups with them in their backpacks. But Summer didn't have the pie they were drooling after. Today she was offering an English toffee cheesecake or Prince William's favorite dessert, Raspberry Eton Mess. They decided on one of each so they could try them both.

Summer sat with them again, and while they had their afternoon treat designed to hold them over for a late dinner, Joan showed Summer all the pictures from the morning trip to the museum. They also talked about the show they were going to attend that evening as Summer hadn't seen it yet.

~***~

Alen and Joan both loved the *United Queendom* production. It was the story, portrayed with humor, of King George II's birthday party and his two loves. His wife, Queen Caroline, and his mistress, Lady Henrietta Howard. Neither woman was one to be trifled with. The period costumes were lovely, but the production itself was hilarious.

After dinner, they returned home. They fed the dogs earlier when they were home, after their walk, and the dogs had already been walked. It was still odd that neither Darcy nor Lizzie greeted them when they came in. Alen went to set the coffee pot for the next morning, and Joan set out to find the dogs. Alen heard her laugh.

"Did you find them?" he called up the stairs.

"Yep, they went to bed without us, and they didn't leave much room for us. I think we might have to sleep in the other room," she answered still laughing when he walked into the room.

"They'll make room for us. You know, tomorrow is Monday, and I desperately feel like I need a weekend. But not another one like this. I'm exhausted. But it was fun," he said.

"I agree. Good night, I have a big day tomorrow. I'm determined to catch a thief."

"Sweet dreams, my feisty bride," Alen said as he drifted off to sleep.

SCARLETT MOSS

Chapter Twenty-Four

Dressed in her disguise, Joan left to watch the museum gift shop, hoping today would be a day that Holly would spend her lunch hour in the gift shop. Joan had studied the museum's interactive map and knew where the gift shop was as well as the fact that there was a gallery directly across from the shop that exhibited garden sculptures. She wondered how long she could spend in there looking at garden sculptures while casing the gift shop. But she also knew that gallery was flanked on either side with portrait and sculpture galleries. The view wouldn't be as good as it was theoretical that she would be too far in a particular direction to see if Holly approached from the opposite side, but she would just have to do the best she could. She was almost wishing they had bought Alen a disguise so he could help. But like he kept reminding her yesterday, the goal was to be as inconspicuous as possible, and two people loitering for hours in a single gallery would be even more suspicious and noticeable as one. At this moment, she was thinking the distinctive black and silver hair probably wasn't her best idea. The typical lunch hour in London was from 12:00 p.m. to 1:30 p.m., with most workers only taking a half hour. Prepared for staggered lunch shifts across departments, she wanted to be in place by 11:30 a.m. and would stay until 2:00 p.m. If she didn't see Holly then, she'd have to return again.

When she'd read that the gallery across the corridor from the gift shop was the garden sculpture gallery, immediately visions of gnomes, bird baths, and casts of woodland animals popped into her head. When she arrived, she was delighted to discover statues of people that were life size or bigger, displays that would obscure her from view if she felt someone was paying too much attention to the woman who studied sculptures like she was looking for a grain of crumbling sandstone. All she needed was to be arrested for stalking or intent to forge a classic piece of art. She also was pleased that this gallery had windows that looked out into the garden. If her Spidey sense was good enough, she could spend some time looking out the windows. But she knew her most important mission was noticing if Holly entered the shop.

After an hour, that seemed like at least four hours, she got her wish. Having already noticed a small chip in the goddess' nose, she was ready to move on to a different sculpture, but this particular display gave her not only perfect cover because it was tall enough to hide Joan, but also gave her almost perfect vision into the glass-fronted gift shop across the way. She spotted the approaching V&A apron first while peeking around a sculpture of Sunna, the Nordic goddess of the sun. She actually was fascinated how the artist was able to make the goddess's curly hair resemble rays of the sun. But right now, her target was in focus. She played off a hunch. If Holly was a kleptomaniac, she wouldn't be able to resist stealing even with the heat on, and the fact that there was someone new manning the gift shop following Greyson's demise added an extra element of excitement. Joan's gamble paid off. While she couldn't see what Holly was looking at specifically, she could see exactly at what point in the aisle she stopped, bent over, and spent some time.

Joan's heart raced. Her palms grew sweaty. She wanted more than anything to pull out her phone and call Alen. But she couldn't. She didn't realize she was holding her breath until a small child bumped into her kneecap and brought her back to the gallery and the goddess she was peeking behind. She realized she likely looked exactly like a stalker. So, she moved around, her eyes focused on the glass windows across the way. When Holly left the gift shop, after spending all her time in one particular spot, it was all Joan could do to keep from running over to the shop. She thought she had figured out how Holly was stealing the artifacts. And if she was right, there was no counting the number of artifacts the woman may have stolen over the twenty-plus years she worked there. She and Grace had already located over a dozen of them, probably close to two dozen. And she realized they had never even looked at Holly's house or her aunt's.

Joan forced herself to walk along the glass front of the shop as though she was just window shopping. What she was actually looking for were cameras. This was a museum; she was sure they would have cameras. She hoped one would be pointed toward the spot where Holly just spent an unusual amount of time. Joan knew there were cameras somewhere, but she couldn't see them. She entered the store as though something in the window intrigued her. She roamed each aisle, occasionally picking up items. She was trying to appear as normal as possible. But she discovered that trying to appear normal felt absolutely conspicuous. Finally, she made her way to the area of the store where Holly looked at an item. It was a small statue. Joan's nerves were beyond frazzled, so she decided to dispense with normalcy and went right to the object at the back of the shelf. She picked it up and turned it over.

There is was...the telltale markings of museum property. She stood there wondering what she should do next. She hadn't discussed that with Alen. But she just realized the critical mistake she made. She had just added her own fingerprints to the item. She realized she had reduced her options of what to do next to two. She could alert museum security or she could call the police. There was a third option she realized. She could purchase the small statue. She could take it home with her and make it disappear. And while that would remove her fingerprints from the puzzle, it would also mean losing vital evidence. Her hands were shaking. Her breathing was labored. And she decided she could take a minute and call Alen. She needed his advice on what to do next.

Joan called Alen. The phone rang and rang. In her adrenaline-fueled nervousness, she forgot that Connie was coming to the shop and Alen was going to record the conversation. When voice mail finally answered she hung up and realized she was on her own.

This is what you wanted, Joanie girl. You wanted to be the investigator. You wanted to get in the middle of this. Alen never did. So, don't be surprised that you're on your own and it's up to you how you handle this, she thought.

Then she had a brilliant idea. If it would work.

She approached the cashier and said, "I would like to buy this item, please. But, I'm curious. What are these numbers inscribed on the bottom?"

"Oh, I'm not really sure. I need to ask my supervisor. I would guess that it's a stock number or something."

"I noticed the others don't have it. Just this one. I thought

Leveled in London

maybe it was a winning promotion or something. Find the item with the secret code, or buy the 325,145th item and get a discount, win a car?" Joan asked hopefully. The cashier laughed.

"No, I don't think it's either of those. I'll set it back here and ask my boss about it when he returns. In the meantime, why don't we get you a clean one to take home," she suggested. Joan followed her to the shelf where she selected the first statue, turned it over and confirmed there was no inscribed number.

Joan breathed a deep sigh of relief, paid for the statue in cash, and quickly left the shop and the museum. She couldn't believe that worked as well as it did. Hopefully, her inquiry would launch an internal investigation and there would be a reason for her fingerprints to be on the statue.

~***~

Meanwhile, Tommy and Grace were having a conversation with Connie Read Burns. Alen was in the upstairs kitchen of Love It or Thrift It, videotaping the meeting taking place below the kitchen. He appeared to be reading emails on his phone and drinking coffee to the people below.

"Thanks for agreeing to meet us here. There's so much going on right now. This is Tommy my husband. Tommy, this is Connie," Grace said.

"Yeah, we met at the Ugly Shakespeare a time or two," Connie replied shaking hands with Tommy.

"I'm going to put up the closed sign and lock the door. Have a seat in the sitting area," Grace instructed.

"So, you want to sell out your inventory and you're closing up your shop?" Tommy asked her. Grace returned and sat on the settee next to him, across from Connie.

"I'm considering it. If the right buyer comes along," Connie answered.

"Did you come up with a price?" Grace asked.

"I did. Here is a spreadsheet listing all of the inventory and its resale value. It comes to $250,000. I'll take $125,000 for it. That gives you a clean retail markup," Connie stated.

"And you said you paid all your consignees for their inventory, correct?" Grace asked.

"Yes. I did," Connie replied.

At that moment, Alen's phone rang silently. He could see Joan was calling, but his phone was on Do Not Disturb so it wouldn't interrupt the video recording. He would have to call her back, and thankfully his subjects were unaware of the call.

"Do you have receipts for those payments or statements from the customers that you paid? I just want to avoid a situation of someone coming into the shop here and saying, 'Hey- that's mine.'" Tommy asked.

"I didn't bring them with me. But if it's necessary, I can provide those, of course. I've bought as much of the inventory as I could before the life insurance check comes in. But I've been assured it will be here today and I'll finish the payments. The only problem is some of my customers may not want their names shared. I'll have to check with them first," Connie replied.

Grace was reading over the inventory list and looked up nodding discreetly to Tommy.

"Okay, we are officially interested. Are you considering other buyers? Is this a bidding war occasion?"

"I'm willing to sell to you today, under one condition. You must assure me that Addison Cotton is no longer part of this business and will in no way benefit from this transaction," Connie said.

"Oh? Why is that?" Tommy asked.

"It's old history. That's all," Connie replied.

"I would love for you to expand on that. I didn't realize you had a history with Addison," Grace said.

"I went to university as an exchange student in the United States. Addison stole my boyfriend. I've not trusted her since."

"Oh, wow, that *is old* history," Grace said. "Is that why you told the police that River saw stolen merchandise in our store and confronted Addison, making her a suspect in his murder?"

"Yes. Not to frame her, but because I didn't trust her. I found the emails where River was proposing merging the stores. He never mentioned it to me. My only thought was that she was trying to steal my business from me now. So, I will only sell to you if you can assure me that she is no longer a partner with you," Connie said.

"We are still in the process of dissolving that partnership. Let me make sure I understand. You are selling us inventory outright. You are not interested in a partnership with us. Correct?"

"Yes, that's correct. If I'm not going to own Upcycled Kingdom, I'm getting out of it altogether. I'll sell you the inventory flat out," Connie replied.

"Okay, well, per your stipulations, we need to conclude our business with Addison and Layne, and then we'll get back to you," Grace said.

They said their goodbyes and let Connie out. Grace turned the sign on the door to open and closed it behind the lying woman.

"I feel like I need a shower," Grace said.

"I really hate this. Declan is such a nice guy. But this woman is apparently a con and a thief," Tommy said. Then he looked upstairs to Alen. "Did you get it all?"

"I did. Wow, I didn't expect her to come right out with it, did you?"

"About siccing the police on Addison? No, I didn't. So, now what? Do we call Sharp and Fox?"

"Yeah, I think so. But first, I have to call Joan. She called in the middle of that. I need to see if she needs something," Alen said as he dialed Joan's number.

~***~

Joan was on the Tube returning home to Alen when her phone rang. Her phone didn't receive the signal underground, so she saw the missed call as she was leaving the station and called him back.

"I'm so sorry, Sweetheart. I was videoing when you called and I couldn't answer. Are you okay?" Alen said when he answered the phone.

"Yes, Honey. I'm on my way home. I'll be there shortly. Did it work? Your video?"

"Yes, we need to call Sharp and Fox. But I wanted to call you first to make sure you're okay."

"I'm fine, but I'll need to talk to them too. Go ahead and call them," Joan said feeling her strength and resolve return. She realized the adrenaline was working out of her system. She had cracked the case of the museum thief. But there were still two murders to solve.

"I love you, Sweetheart," Alen said into the phone.

"I love you too. I hope this is almost over," she replied.

"Me too. See you soon," and the call disconnected.

Chapter Twenty-Five

WHEN INSPECTORS SHARP AND FOX arrived, Grace again turned the store's sign to closed.

"I thought we told you to stay out of this investigation," Sharp said.

"Technically, we aren't investigating. But if something comes to us, should we keep it to ourselves or share it with you?" Alen asked.

"Fine. What do you have?" Fox asked.

"As we told you, Connie offered to sell us her inventory," Grace said. "We met with her today, and Alen recorded the meeting, you know, just in case something weird happened. And it did. First, the inventory list that she brought us contained a number of the items I noticed in her store on Friday had museum tags. So, we assume you haven't inspected the shop yet. We made a deal to buy the inventory and it is our full intent when we take possession, if those items are still in the collection, we will turn them over to you. We don't want there to be any question that we intended to buy stolen artifacts. Secondly, she confesses in the video why she sent you to talk to Addison."

Alen handed his phone to Sharp and pressed the play button on the video. When the conversation ended, Sharp asked, "Okay. Duly noted. But what exactly do you want us to do with this? It's not admissible if she didn't know she was being recorded."

"I know," Alen said, "But we wanted you to know that the reason she sent you here to talk to Addison wasn't because there was any reason for Addison or Layne or any of us, for that matter, to have harmed River Read."

"Okay. Understood. Anything else?" Shark asked.

"Well, actually, yes, there is," Joan said. "I just happened to be at the museum today and I saw Holly Hunt enter the gift shop. She hovered in an area for a while. After she left, I went to confirm my suspicions. I think you'll likely be able to find video footage from the museum's CC system. She brings the small items that the shop sells replicas of to the shop, hidden under her apron. She places the original item at the very back of the shop's inventory and leaves. She then comes back later and purchases the," Joan air-quoted the next word, "'replica taking home the original artifact. Maisy told us that Greyson told her that Holly had a peculiar habit of always buying the piece at the back of the display. I suspected I knew why and today I was able to confirm it. But after I pulled the item from the back and checked for the museum marking, I panicked, realizing I had just added my fingerprints to the statue. So, I asked the clerk about the numbers as I was purchasing the item. She replaced it with another statue and said she would ask her boss about it. I'm sure that will set off all the appropriate alarms at the museum and she'll be caught. I suspect she may suffer from kleptomania. That doesn't necessarily make her a murderer. But there does seem to be a connection between her and Greyson Cooper. Maisy Cooper told us he had been infatuated with her for years. Though we've found no connection between her and Upcycled Kingdom, other than that Maisy sold items there that Holly gave her aunt, who then passed them down to Maisy."

"Thank you, Mrs. Arny. We'll look into all of this. And now...will you please leave it to us? You're off the hook, okay? Is that what you needed to hear to leave all this alone?" Sharp asked.

"Are Addison and Layne Cotton also off the hook?" Alen asked.

"Yes, yes, okay. We already knew they weren't involved," Fox answered.

"Fine, that's all we needed was to know, it was safe for them to return and that we aren't in any danger either," Alen said. "But could we ask a small favor?"

"What?" Fox asked, without the snark and disdain clear from his previous visits.

"When you discover who the killer is, if Joan and I are still here, would you let us know who it is?"

"Sure, it will be in the paper," Sharp answered.

"Thank you," Alen said, not sure if that meant they should read about it in the paper or the inspector would let them know.

They all bid the inspectors farewell and hoped the only other time they would need to see them would be after the murderer was caught.

The two couples decided to celebrate by going to the London Eye, the observation wheel on the River Thames. Joan lamented that she hadn't captured nearly enough photos of London. It would be dark by the time they got there, but there would still be beautiful photos opportunities. They also managed to get seats on the London by Night bus tour.

They followed up with a late-night dinner at the Ugly Shakespeare. Joan noticed Grace fiddling with her phone. An unusual sight, especially during a meal. Declan was hanging around the table, telling tales about past Burns' Night celebrations. The man was more excited about the event than most children were about Christmas and Santa Claus. Tommy was having the most fun, needling him about the simultaneous events this year of Lightopia London and the big Chinese New Year celebration. Though the couples had already worked out how to enjoy them all, Tommy's fun was in making Declan think they might not come to the big event.

"Is everything okay?" she leaned over and asked Grace quietly.

"Yes, everything is fine. I've just received an email from Addison. I'll tell you about it later."

After dinner, Tommy and Grace walked Joan and Alen home so she could share with them Addison's email and the decisions the two shop owners had made throughout the day.

"I didn't want to bring this up in front of Declan. Not yet anyway. Addison and I have been discussing our plans for the shop via email. She and Layne are coming back early. But they want you to stay for the rest of your scheduled days here. You can stay at the house with them, or if you aren't comfortable, they will put you up in a hotel. But they hope to spend some more time with you and get to know you better. In the meantime, we decided we don't want you to work the shop hours anymore," Grace said.

Before she could finish, Joan was worried, "Did we do something wrong?" she asked.

"On the contrary, we're are so thankful for all your help, we just want you to have fun. We know you canceled some of your activities. Spend the rest of the time here doing whatever you want, whenever you want. Tommy and I will cover the store hours, or if we can't, we'll close. It's not a big deal."

"What about Connie? If she finds out Addison and Layne are coming back, she won't sell to you," Alen reminded her.

"It doesn't matter. I truly couldn't care less whether we buy her inventory or not. It's up to her, it's not going to make or break us either way."

"Okay, so Addison and Layne think it's safe to come back, even though the murders aren't solved?" Joan asked.

"Yeah, I think it's just a matter of time. They didn't do it. We didn't do it. If it's the same murderer, they couldn't have done it, since Greyson was murdered while they were in the U.S. So, go in there and plan a day of fun or something relaxing for tomorrow, okay? I'll be here in the morning to open the shop."

"Well, okay. Thank you! Do you know when Addison and Layne will be back?" Joan asked.

"Not yet, she's checking on changing her tickets, I'll likely hear back from her tomorrow."

SCARLETT MOSS

Chapter Twenty-Six

THE NEXT MORNING, ALEN AND JOAN had a leisurely morning for the first day since arriving in London. Joan had told the dog walkers the previous evening that they didn't need to come this morning for the morning walk. While they enjoyed their evenings with Lizzie and Darcy and the playful game they still played every morning to get the dogs out of the bed, Joan felt they weren't as close to the dogs as they got to Sherlock with their daily walks. While it was nice to not have to walk them several times a day, she was surprised to discover she missed the activity.

They took the dogs and walked the few blocks to the embankment along the River Thames to an area called Champion's Wharf. They came upon an area with a modern sculpture called Pope's Urn. The sculpture was crafted from drawings of an urn the poet Alexander Pope designed in the 1800's for a friend's garden. Encircling the sculpture were benches with quotes from Pope's poems that are now common phrases. Alen pointed one out to Joan. They were walking as they almost always did, hand in hand, each carrying a leash attached to one of the dogs in their charge. Joan held Darcy's leash; Alen held Lizzie's.

"Look Sweetheart, a passage of wisdom to us by a poet from ages ago. He apparently could see into the future." Alen pointed to one of the inscribed benches facing the urn sculpture. It read, *Fools rush in where angels fear to tread.* Joan cut her eyes at him as if to say, really?

"Oh wait, this one was written especially for you," he said pointing to another. It read; *A little learning is a dangerous thing.*

"Alen Arny, you are not even a little bit funny! I solved a crime this week. Almost all on my own. At least the police aren't looking at Addison and Layne as suspects, and they can come home to these furry loves. They aren't looking at us as suspects, and we will make it to our next house-sitting obligation. Now, we also have time to enjoy London! I think you should be thanking me," she retorted.

"My queen, thou art my queen, my thanks to ye," he teased back.

Joan was standing in front of a bench that faced the water and she motioned for him. "Here. This is our bench. Let's sit. I want to get some outdoor pictures of the dogs too." Alen and Lizzie walked over. Alen read the back of the bench.

"I agree. This one is perfect," Alen replied as he sat down on the bench that was inscribed, *To wake the soul by tender strokes of art.*

"And, Sweetheart, not only do I adore you as I have since the day that I met you, but I'm proud of you. You did do the thing here. You were smart, organized, and you did it all safely. I'm very impressed. But I've also made an important decision," Alen said.

"You made an important decision, without me?" she asked him, while snapping photos. He took a minute to see if there were men in kilts around before he continued, given her propensity for snapping photos of any man in a kilt.

"I did. We agreed when we decided to embark on this adventure that we were going to try new things,"

"Yes, we did. And you're learning to cook. And I'm not sure if there is anything in the world hotter than a man in an apron in the kitchen. But what is your decision?"

"I know I was kind of a pill about this investigation. I didn't want any part of it. I retired from law enforcement, and I wanted to leave it all behind me. Yes, I'm learning to cook. And you aptly pointed out that solving crimes was new to you, and you went about it on your own, like I did the cooking. But I failed to see an important part of the picture," he explained.

"Yes, handsome. What is that?"

"That solving crimes with you is new to me. Doing it together is different. And from now on, when we find ourselves in the middle of a crime scene, I want us to work together. Like we did in Edinburgh. Not because a little learning is a dangerous thing. Not because you aren't perfectly capable of doing it on your own, but because I enjoy doing it with you. So, I won't be a pill about it anymore. You can always count on me," he said while absently stroking Lizzie's head.

Joan, finished snapping pictures in this spot, came over and sat on the bench next to Alen. He put his arm around her.

"That's lovely, Honey. You're welcome to join in on my cases whenever you like, and I'll enjoy working with you. But there's one important thing you should know," she said.

"Oh, what? That you're in charge now?" he asked with a sarcastic undertone.

"No. You're welcome to crime-solve with me, just don't expect me to cook with you, okay?" They both laughed.

"Deal!"

They walked the dogs over to the fountain and let them off their leashes. Joan wanted to get pictures of them interacting together without the tethers. They didn't disappoint as they frolicked with the splashing water in the background and then together dipped their noses in for a small drink before returning to Joan and Alen, getting their leashes back on and continuing on their walk. Later when she looked at the photos of the dogs around the fountain, she giggled at how they blended in with the sculptures surrounding it. She decided this was the photo she would have printed and framed to leave with Addison and Layne. They took the dogs home and headed into the city to take a tour they decided to splurge on at the last minute.

Joan had planned on the Sherlock Holmes walking tour. But in the meantime, had discovered a tour that combined Sherlock Holmes with other British icons. It was called the Bard, Beatles, Bond, & Baker Street tour. They would be driven around in a classic black taxi for three hours on this tour instead of walking. The tour covered Shakespeare, Sherlock Holmes, Sir Arthur Conan Doyle, Ian Fleming, James Bond and the Beatles. It was by far the most expensive tour, but it turned out to be worth every penny.

When the tour ended, Joan counted silently in her head the seconds until she heard Alen's standard refrain.

"That was fun, thanks Sweetheart for finding that tour. I'm hungry. Where's lunch?"

They returned to a restaurant they had seen near the Monument to the Great Fire of London called Olive and Squash.

Alen ordered a citrus salad with fried rosemary and olives, and Joan decided on a spinach and squash salad with coconut dressing. After lunch they decided they had enough energy left to go on the Crown Jewels and Tower of London tour. While Joan had dismissed seeing the castles and palaces when they were investigating at the Victoria and Albert museum, Alen knew she really wanted to see the Crown Jewels.

On the tour, Joan and Alen not only marveled at the beauty of the more than 23,000 jewels, but learned the history of them, how these were not the original crown jewels, what happened to the originals, and the meaning and process of a coronation. They also enjoyed the ceremonial robes and other items including the Grand Punch Bowl that holds 144 bottles of wine.

They were walking to the Underground tube station, walking hand in hand. Relaxed and happy. Like tourist should be.

"For a country so small, that's a lot of jewels to belong to one person," Alen said.

"Well, they don't really belong to the Queen, they belong to the monarchy. So, it's more like they belong to the country in a way," she answered. "However, I do think I need a crown! I could be the Queen of International Crime," she said.

A well-dressed man in a suit was walking quickly past them, but as she said that, his step faltered and his head swiveled back. Apparently, he decided she didn't look too dangerous, and she and Alen both laughed. She tried to explain, but she was laughing too hard, and the man hurried on his way again.

"I'm not sure if that's a compliment or an insult. It's like he heard the words, thought oh crap looked at me and thought, she's no harm," Joan said indignantly.

"Could you be happy to be my queen? Let's leave any reference to crime out of it," Alen suggested.

"Okay, can I still have the crown?" she asked.

"It won't fit in the suitcase," he reminded her.

"I could wear it on the plane. Wouldn't we make a memorable couple. Me, the red headed queen and you, the sexy kilt apron wearing chef."

"No. Absolutely not, that's not happening," he said. Though to Joan's ears, he didn't sound all that convincing.

They returned to the shop and Grace was still there. The long hours were beginning to take a toll on her and she looked fatigued.

"Addison and Layne will be here tomorrow. Their flight gets in at 10:00 a.m. Do you want to stay here at the house, or would you like me to make you reservations somewhere else?" she asked.

"No, there's no need for that. We can stay here, if that's okay with Addison and Layne. I hate they felt the need to cut their trip short."

"They were hoping you would choose to stay here. They really want to spend some time with you. I think honestly, they were ready to come home. They spent a lot of time with her sister, attended the wedding they went for, and I think they miss the dogs. And their life here. She also mentioned wanting to be here for Burns' Night. If we are going to Declan's, we should make a reservation for six," she answered.

"Is Tommy going to go?" Alen asked, referring to Tommy's constant teasing Declan.

"Yes, he's going to go. Lightopia London lasts for weeks. In fact, we could go tomorrow night if you like. If Addison and Layne aren't too tired, they could go with us. And the best part of the Chinese New Year is the parade, in the daytime and it's the next day. Isn't that how most holidays are? Busy, busy, a lot of work, and then some fun. Then curling up with a good book to relax with."

"That sounds good. Tomorrow, I'm going to see if Declan will give me some more cooking lessons, or maybe I can pop in early to the Mug Shot and see what Summer is cooking up in the morning." Alen said.

"To be honest, a quiet day with a book sounds heavenly," Joan said. "But I could help with the store tomorrow. I think we need a break from the tours."

"We decided to close the shop for the week. We all need a rest. So, it will be really quiet for you tomorrow until Layne and Addison get here, probably around eleven, unless there are flight delays. Why don't we all get together for lunch?"

"Okay, great, we'll see you then," Joan said. And Grace left.

"I'm thinking. Alen, if you go to Mug Shot at 6 a.m. to bake, you could bring me breakfast in bed. I could laze around reading until time to get dressed for Addison's and Layne's arrival and lunch. I think that's absolutely what a good husband learning to cook would do," Joan teased Alen.

"Well, the thing is, now that you mention it, a morning lazing around with my wife sounds like as much fun as learning to bake," he teased back.

SCARLETT MOSS

Chapter Twenty-Seven

JOAN WAS SLOWLY GAINING CONSCIOUSNESS but she felt as if she was floating on a cloud. She turned in the bed, realizing she met with no resistance. Opening her eyes, she realized she was in the big fluffy bed all alone. Alen and both dogs were missing. Her cloudy brain thought, *what a wonderful man. He's gotten the dogs up already for their walk. And somehow without waking me. He's so sweet...* And just like that, she was back into a deep sleep.

The next time she awoke, the bedroom door was opening and she could smell the pungent aroma of that energy-giving elixir she loved. Coffee. She rolled over and opened her eyes just as the sensation of two large trees falling across the bed indicated that Lizzie and Darcy were back. And standing in the doorway was her husband. Wearing the apron she bought him in Edinburgh with a bare-chested hunk wearing a kilt printed on it. Even better, he was holding a tray with a mug of steaming coffee. She smiled at him and sat up so he could place the tray on her lap once the dogs settled into their spots. Alongside the coffee was a bowl. It appeared to be something creamy with odd fruit on top.

"This smells really good, what is it?" she asked.

"It's called tea-poached dried fruit and it's served over yogurt. It's what I made at the Mug Shot this morning," he answered proudly.

"Wait. You already went to Mug Shots, made something and are back home? What time is it?"

"Nine o'clock. You were sleeping well. I fed the dogs already. Look, they're ready for a morning nap with you already," he answered. She took a sip of coffee first, then a bite of the fruit and yogurt.

"This is really good. What did you say it is?" she asked him.

He laughed. He knew her well enough to know that nothing stuck in her brain before her early morning coffee. Now that she had her first sip and was working on more waiting for his reply he answered her.

"It's dried fruit, steeped in tea to reconstitute it. Pretty nifty, huh?" he explained.

"Yes. It's a unique flavor. I like it. So much for a lazy morning reading in bed. I suppose I should get up and get ready for Addison and Layne to get home. I feel like I should clean something. Or cook something. There's something I should be doing before they come back, right?"

"Mrs. White cleaned. Addison doesn't cook. They don't eat here. I did bring some scones from The Tea's Knees and put them in the kitchen in case anyone needs something. I think everything is fine. While you shower, I'll sweep up downstairs and when you get down, you can make some coffee for them," he answered. He could have easily made the coffee, but he understood she was a little nervous about their return and wanted, needed something to do.

~***~

Tommy and Grace arrived first. They were all sitting in the residence living room. Suddenly Lizzie and Darcy jumped up and began howling. Alen and Joan had not ever heard them howl and were startled. Tommy and Grace laughed at the dogs who were now standing by the door to the alley, jumping, prancing, and howling.

"Mum and Dad are here," Grace explained just before the door opened. Addison came in first and kneeled down just inside the doorway to hug both of her fur babies. The dogs licked her face and continued to wiggle until Layne was inside too and petting them.

"What a happy reunion," Joan said. She and Alen were smiling, watching them greeting their humans. Alen realized they didn't bring in their luggage.

"Can I get your luggage for you?" he asked.

"It's okay. I'll get it," Layne answered, "We knew though there was no sense in you having to listen to the howling while we wrestled with it, and trying to get it in the door with excited dogs usually proves futile anyway."

"Yes, we are so happy to be home, too…" Addison was cooing to the dogs.

"We haven't heard them howl before now. A single welcome woof has been about it, except for the first day when the cops beat on the door. And that was full on barking,"

"They only howl when we come back from an overnight trip," Layne explained.

Addison stood up and walked over to sit on the sofa. "We are so very sorry you've been having to deal with all this. If we had any idea, we wouldn't have left you here. But I suppose you have a story to tell within the house sitter community, huh? I bet we'll be blacklisted and never be able to get another house sitter. Anyway, I didn't mean for that to sound like it was about us. It isn't. Again, I'm so sorry," she said to Alen and Joan.

"Don't be silly. There was no way you could know someone was going to murder..." before she could continue there was a loud rap on the door.

Lizzie and Darcy barked furiously. It appeared their opinion was there were quite enough people in the house already.

Addison held on to a dog collar in each hand while Layne opened the door.

"Who are you?" said a male voice outside.

"I'm Layne Cotton. Who are you?" Layne answered.

"Mr. Cotton, the prodigal shop owner. Welcome back to London. I'm DCI Sharp and my partner DCI Fox from the city of London police. We talked on the phone," Sharp said.

"Yes, sir. I recall. Come in. Does the city of London Police have our passports flagged or something? What can we do for you today?"

"No, sir," Fox answered shaking his hand. "We didn't know you would be here. That's why we asked who you were. We know the Arnys and the Bells."

Sharp approached Addison, who was still sitting on the couch holding on to the dogs. He held out a hand to her. "Mrs. Addison Cotton, I presume?"

"Do you really want me to let go of the dogs to shake your hand?"

"Yes, ma'am. We know they're harmless. Beautiful dogs, by the way," he complimented warmly when she let go of Darcy and shook his hand.

"We came to update you on the case, as we promised we would," Fox said.

"Oh, something happened?" Alen asked.

Leveled in London

"Yes. It seems Mrs. Arny, you cracked the case," Fox said.

"You mean the theft of the museum items, right?" Joan asked.

"That and the murders of River Read and Greyson Cooper," Sharp answered. "We brought Holly Hunt in for questioning after observing the video footage of the gift shop at the Victoria and Albert Museum. The museum has above par security footage, and while she was very good at it, and managed to not trigger suspicion until you witnessed her actions and alerted the store clerk, they had footage going back and we were able to figure out her pattern. It appears she has stolen no less than several hundred items while working at the museum. We also found items at her home, the home of Lady Klara Pearce, and the Upcycled Kingdom shop," Sharp explained.

"It appears your diagnosis of kleptomania was correct as well. Ms. Hunt seemed almost relieved to be caught. But during questioning, we learned what happened to River Read and Greyson Cooper," Fox added.

"Oh, no, tell me she didn't murder those men," Joan said. "She seemed like a nice lady, if troubled."

"Actually, Greyson Cooper killed River Read. Mr. Read attempted to call Maisy Cooper to let her know he suspected some of the items she consigned with him were stolen. Greyson intercepted the call. He called his mother and asked where she got the items she consigned. She told him they were from Lady Klara Pearce, gifts from Holly that the woman didn't want. Greyson figured out that Holly was the source. He apparently has been enamored with the woman for some time. He went to talk to Read to try to convince him to let him take the items out of the store without alerting the police. The man refused and there was a scuffle. The large monstrance fell from a pedestal and struck Read in the head after he was already on the ground from the fight. Cooper fled the scene, not aware that the man was dying," Sharp explained.

"When he heard the news that the man was dead, Cooper confronted Holly and told her that he was trying to defend her and in the course of that action killed a man," Fox said.

"He then called her when you called him and wanted to talk and told her it wasn't over. She was in his garden watching you all when you were there. She realized that, if she killed him, you all would be suspects and she would remain undiscovered. At least, that's how she foresaw it all going down," Sharp finished.

"She was there at his house when we were there? So, if we had noticed her, we might have saved his life?" Grace asked.

"No, ma'am. Don't think like that. Actually, you're all very lucky. She might have killed all of you," Fox answered.

"So, it's all over?" Addison asked.

"Except for the audience and possibly an investiture ceremony," Fox teased.

"A what?" Tommy asked.

"The museum is thankful for your assistance and has nominated Mrs. Arny for an award from the Sovereign. The Queen," Sharp explained. "Her Majesty is requesting an audience with Mr. and Mrs. Arny. Though the next award investiture ceremony won't take place until the summer, after her birthday celebration. I'm sure she'll ask if it's possible for you to return to London."

"The queen wants to meet me?" Joan asked surprised.

"Yes, ma'am. And the museum has asked me to give you this cheque, a small reward, as a token of their appreciation," Fox said holding out a check for Joan.

"But but I can't possibly meet the queen. I have nothing to wear for an event like that," she protested. She looked around at her new friends. She was clearly in shock.

"That's okay, Sweetheart. I know where we can get you something to wear. When will this meeting take place?"

"At 11 a.m. on Monday," Sharp answered. The palace will get in touch with you shortly to confirm," Sharp answered. "We would also like to thank you for your help. We hope you have a pleasurable time in our city." He shook Joan's hand, then Alen's hand, and then turned to go out the door. Fox followed behind.

Joan stood in the middle of the room. Numb.

Once the inspectors were safely out the door, the room erupted in cheers for their new friend.

SCARLETT MOSS

Chapter Twenty-Eight

ADDISON, LAYNE, TOMMY, GRACE, AND Alen all stood around Joan. They whooped, woo-hooed, and applauded for their friend. Lizzie and Darcy joined in. Sitting at each of Joan's feet, they pointed their long snoots into the air and howled for their honorary aunt.

"Am I dreaming?" Joan asked. Her hand went to her mouth and covered it as she tried to absorbed what just happened. "The queen wants to meet me? What does that even mean? I don't think I want to do it. What will I say? What will I wear?"

"Joan, Sweetheart. This is a good thing. You'll get a photo of you with the Queen," Alen said, knowing the idea of a photo might bring her around.

"Oh, Alen, people will just think it's a photo from Madame Tussaud's," she said as they all sat back down.

"We need to celebrate! What would you like to do?"

Addison asked.

"We talked about going to Lightopia London this evening if you and Layne felt up to it after your trip," Grace mentioned.

"Sure! I'm so excited, there's no way I could sleep," Addison said.

"But I'm starving…" Layne said. The whole room erupted into laughter again.

"What?" he asked.

"That's Alen's line," Tommy said. "Alen is always hungry."

"And Alen is starving too, let's go get some lunch," Alen said.

They all walked down to The Ugly Shakespeare. Declan greeted them and was excited to see Layne and Addison were back.

"We're celebrating," Layne told him. "And we're famished. Our friend Joan here has been invited for an audience with Her Majesty and has been rewarded by the museum. The case is officially closed. We can all sleep better now that the killer has been caught. I'm sure Connie feels better, now too."

"They caught River's killer? They haven't told us yet. Connie's upstairs. I'll ring her and have her come down. We have a Rabbit Pie and Mash or Shepherd's Pie for the lunch special today, while you decide, I'll get coffee all around, right?"

"Yes," they all answered.

When Connie arrived, Layne told them all the story. Addison and Connie looked at each other often and warily. But neither one mentioned their past.

"Tomorrow we are going shopping," Addison said.

"All of us?" Alen asked nervously. The other two men shifted in their seats, uncomfortably.

"Gawd, no. Grace, Joan, and I," Addison said. Then looked at Grace. A twinkle appeared in both their eyes…

"Bond Street, here we come," they said in unison.

"But tonight, we go to Lightopia London and celebrate the festival of light."

"You are all coming to Burns' Night, right?" Declan asked.

"Yes, we are all coming," Layne answered. "So, reserve us a table for six. Eight if you and Connie can join us." And with that statement, everyone relaxed. The long-hanging hatchet between Addison and Connie was buried.

"We need to take the tube to Lightopia as there is only a small car park and it's reserved for disabled attendees. So, let's plan to leave at four," Grace said.

"Addison, Layne, do you need to rest before we go?" Tommy asked.

"No, but I do want to get our luggage in and unpack. I have gifts for you all," Addison said. "Unless you have something else to do, you may as well just stay with us until time to go."

"Sure, we can stay," Tommy said. "I'm anxious to see what you brought back," as they walked back to the house.

They closed the electric shades on the front of the store. Grace, Tommy, Alen, and Joan sat around the big table in the kitchen overlooking the shop while Addison and Layne unpacked. Lizzie and Darcy were glued to their humans.

Addison returned with both a small suitcase in tow and a shopping bag. Lizzie and Darcy were following her. She sat down at the table and pulled out a pink flamingo and a purple unicorn squeaky dog toys for Lizzie and Darcy. Lizzie grabbed the purple unicorn first and Darcy went for the flamingo, and they ran into the living room with their toys. She then pulled out two items wrapped in colorful stripped tissue paper.

"I know you guys don't have room in your suitcases for much. But I wanted to bring you something to express our appreciation for all you've done and been through while you were here. I never dreamed this would be a traumatic experience," she said handing a package to each Joan and Alen.

"It wasn't traumatic at all, and you didn't need to do this," Joan said unwrapping her package. "But I'm so glad you did!" Inside was a pair of red socks, each one imprinted with a goldendoodle on it that looked exactly like Lizzie and Darcy.

"Thank you, I love them. And I'll always remember Lizzie and Darcy," she said, getting up and hugging Addison.

Alen unwrapped his package and laughed. It was an apron that said, 'Not all Superheroes wear capes…some wear aprons. "Thank you, Addison. This one I could wear on a plane and not be embarrassed!" they all laughed.

Then Addison laid down the small suitcase and unzipped it. As she did, she said, "And this is for our best friends ever!" She flipped bag the lid to expose a suitcase full of American products not available in the U.K. Grace and Tommy rifled through it to discover plastic zipper bags, dryer sheets, Cheetos, Kraft Mac & Cheese, grits, Hershey's Kisses, Cheez-Its, saltine crackers, and creamy peanut butter.

Then they all left to go experience the wonder of Lightopia, a light and lantern festival at Chiswick House and Gardens. As they walked through the gardens, they experienced light displays, acrobatic and musical performers all celebrating life. When they reached the exit at the end of the exhibition and started walking back toward the underground, Alen spoke up.

"Hey, you guys…" he said. But before he could finish everyone in the group finished the sentence for him…

"You're starving!" They all laughed, and then Addison and Layne insisted they were treating everyone to dinner at The Grapes.

"What's The Grapes?" Alen asked.

"You'll see." Addison teased.

The Grapes, it turned out, was a famous pub established in 1583 and appears in the opening paragraph of Charles Dickens' novel *Our Mutual Friend*. The pub is now owned by Sir Ian McKellen, who played Gandalf in the *Lord of the Rings* movies. Downstairs is a traditional English pub, and in the back parlor a bookcase is home to a complete library of Charles Dickens' works. Upstairs is an elegant dining room with crisp white tablecloths and crystal stemware on the tables. The pub has a long bar leading to the back parlor called the Dickens Snug, and a heated terrace that overhangs the river. The three couples enjoyed their dinner as if they were lifelong friends. Which they all felt they would be from this point forward. Inevitably conversation wound around to Joan's audience with the queen.

"I don't suppose I can wear my new socks to meet the queen, right?" she asked.

"Right," Alen said emphatically.

"I don't know. I think she might can," Addison said. "If she wears boots."

"I've been thinking about it. I realize I need a dress. That facilitates shoes. Alen needs a suit. And also, shoes. I suppose I need a proper purse. I hate having to buy all this and then not have room to take it with us. Boots would really take up a lot of room in the suitcase. But leaving it all behind seems like a crazy waste of money, for what…twenty minutes with the queen? I'm thinking of not going," Joan said to her new friends.

"You're crazy!" Tommy said.

"You have to go!" Addison said.

"Oh, yes, you are, you deserve this," Alen said.

"Joan, you need to do this for yourself," Grace said.

All at once. The table had erupted in the elegant dining room.

Joan was overwhelmed again.

"And for your country, and women the world over. This is such an honor. And you deserve it, like your proud husband said. We'll figure out the suitcase thing," Grace said compassionately.

"I know it's terrifying. But we're all here for you. Grace and I will help you with the shopping and the packing. If you don't want to take the clothes, we'll donate them to charity," Addison suggested.

"I'm sure between us, Addison and I have jewelry and accessories you can borrow. For that matter, we probably have a dress you could borrow, but you deserve something that is perfectly you for this day. This is truly a rare occasion. And one so many long for," Grace said.

"Okay. I guess nerves are getting the better of me. Thanks, y'all," she said, still not sounding convinced.

When they left the restaurant, they decided to take taxis home instead of the underground. So, they bid Tommy and Grace goodbye at the restaurant.

Chapter Twenty-Nine

TOMMY AND GRACE ARRIVED AT 9:30 a.m. Everyone was ready to go. But first, they went to The Tea's Knees for breakfast. Fern was excited to see that Addison and Layne were back.

"What are you all up to today?" Fern asked.

"Grace and I are taking Joan shopping. She has an audience with her Royal Majesty!" Addison told her.

"Oh, my, how lucky you are! I would be a blathering mess if it were me," Fern said.

"We are going cart racing while they shop," Layne said.

"I hope you all have a fun day," she wished them as they left to go their separate ways.

The ladies went to Bond street first. They visited several stores like Akris, Christian Dior, Givenchy, Ferragamo, and Joan good naturedly tried on dresses from the outlandish to couture. None of them seemed right, even if she ignored the over £1,000 price tags that threatened to give her hives. The check the museum sent more than covered all their expenses thus far in London. Especially since Layne and Addison covered the majority of their eating expenses. And Alen had told her not to worry about the money. Find something she felt good in and splurge on herself for once. He was so proud of her. But she decided to come clean and be honest with her new friends.

"You know, this has actually been fun. Even though I've always despised shopping. But I have to be honest. It makes me weak in the knees to see these price tags. I know it's a special event. But the reality is, it's something I'm probably going to wear one time. And then maybe even give it away. It just feels irresponsible to spend this much. Is there somewhere we can shop that's more modest? Where I can find something appropriate but feel more comfortable with?"

"Yes," Grace said understanding. "We didn't think you would actually buy something here. But we wanted you to have fun, feel special. Because you are."

"Wait. I just don't want to go to Harrod's, okay? While I love their shopping bags, that's too big. Too many choices," Joan clarified.

"How about Selfridge's?" Addison asked.

"Perfect," Grace answered.

"Oh, I loved that TV show about Selfridge's. Yes, please. Let's go there. I should be able to find a dress, some shoes, and even a suit for Alen all in one place. Thanks, girls. You're like the best BFFs ever!"

"We can even have lunch there too," Addison added.

Joan found the perfect dress and knee-high black boots, a suit, dress shirt, tie, and shoes for Alen. Noticing tartans displayed throughout the store, she finally caught the shopping bug.

Leveled in London

"If I'm splurging on clothes we'll likely never wear again, I might as well splurge on something fun to wear to Burns' Night too!"

"That's it, yeah, now we're having fun!" Addison said.

She found a red tartan turtleneck for herself that would go with her black jeans for the night, and a watch plaid tartan shirt for Alen. But by the time it was all totaled up it was just under £1,500. Joan had graduated. By taking her to Bond street first, where many of the price tags on the dresses she tried on were over £3,000, she felt she had done well. And everyone was happy.

Then they went to San Carlo on the Selfridge's rooftop for lunch, where they all decided on the Duck Salad. Joan had to admit, the lifestyle of the rich and famous wasn't all that bad.

Over lunch, Addison and Grace informed Joan that tomorrow they were taking her to their favorite spa for the day. She started to protest and then decided to just go with it.

"What all do you still want to see in London while you're here?" Addison asked.

"So much. So so so much. It feels like we haven't even made a drop in the bucket yet. We've already decided we need to come back again next year. We're resigned to not seeing it all," she answered.

"Tommy and I were discussing a trip to the Greek Islands next year. We would need someone to house and dog sit. Would you consider sitting for us?"

"We would love to, as long as you promise not to kill a business associate before you go," she said. They all chuckled, and she asked, "Too soon?"

Addison and Grace both nodded, that yes, it was too soon.

"When you decide, just let me know the dates and we'll book around it," she said.

When they got home, they found Alen as excited as a toddler at Christmas.

"What's going on? Did you have fun?" Joan asked him.

"I did, but I found something we just have to do! We can go this afternoon if you want," he said.

Joan was exhausted from all the trying on and shopping. Especially because it wasn't her favorite thing to do. But seeing how excited Alen was, she didn't have the heart to tell him no, no matter what it was.

"Sure, what is it?"

"An escape room! It's called *The Game is Now: Sherlock*. And teams of six can play, so we can all go. What do say?"

Joan looked to Addison and Grace, who both nodded yes.

"Can we get a cappuccino and a snack first? …I'm starving," Joan teased.

"Sure! Do you want me to go get it takeaway and bring it here? You can put your feet up and show me what's in those bags too."

"That would be delightful. Thank you, Honey," she said. He bounded out of the room to the kitchen, where he collected six travel mugs, and headed down to Mug Shot's. When he returned, he had a selection of desserts, cut them all in half and placed them on a platter and brought the tray Summer loaned him and placed it all on the coffee table. While they dug in to the desserts, he dove into the shopping bags. He loved the dress and boots Joan bought for herself and was happy with the suit, tie, and shoes, but was really excited that they had tartans to wear for Burns' Night.

They took the underground to the escape room game. As they waited to get in, Joan couldn't help herself, she just had to tease Alen.

"So, let me get this straight. This is a game where we are

racing against the clock, we have to find clues and solve puzzles to advance to the next room and ultimately escape?" Joan asked.

"Right," he answered.

"And basically, we are supposed to adapt the character of Sherlock Holmes?" she asked.

"By George, I think she's got it," he said proudly to their friends.

"And, now tell me, Honey. How is this different from being sheriff? You know that thing you don't want to do anymore?" she asked smartly.

"Because I'm doing it with a cast of friends. And since my wife has an audience with the Queen, I'm sure they'll let us out of here before Monday, even if we fail miserably. But we'll have fun in the process," he answered.

"Good answer. Okay, let's go have some fun."

They did have fun. Friendships built on how well they worked together and how they complimented each other. And when they were finally released from the room, they all took a deep breath and in unison declared, "I'm starving."

All the younger people participating in the game looked at the old folks laughing, holding hands, happy and loving. They were quite noticeable and if they were honest, those young people were hoping to be just like them when they grew old.

Grace and Tommy headed home, Addison, Layne, Joan, and Alen did too, by way of The Ugly Shakespeare.

"Is my sous chef available for tomorrow? We are running out of time to prepare for Burns' Night!" Declan said as he served them dinner.

Alen looked questioningly at Joan. She nodded.

"Apparently, my new best friends are hauling me to the spa. They seem to think I need a radical makeover before making the acquaintance of Her Majesty," she answered. Alen looked startled.

"That's not true!" Addison exclaimed. "You are more than adequate, you're perfect, in fact. We just thought a little pampering is deserved. You can choose what you want and what you don't, a manicure, pedicure, massage, sauna, facial, hair treatment. All or none of it. Whatever your heart desires. We should just go, relax, drink mimosas, have a girl's day. That's all. Then we are going to lay out jewelry and accessories for you to choose from for your Royal ensemble," she explained.

"I was just teasing," Joan said sweetly. "I know you didn't mean any of that. And to be honest, I can't remember the last time I had a girl's day. I appreciate it and I'm excited about it. I didn't mean anything other than teasing," she answered.

"Well, good." Alen teased back, "Because I think she's perfect the way she is, and if she comes back looking like a European uptown girl that I don't recognize, she might ditch me for a man in a kilt."

"I might do that anyway, Honey," she replied, and they all laughed.

"Be sure and bring your camera to Burns' Night," Declan said.

"I will. And I bought Alen and I tartans to wear for the occasion," Joan told him.

"I'm flattered, I am. Alen, I plan to start with the Sticky Puddings in the morning. Come for breakfast before you go for your girl's day. Have a fine evening, my friends."

Alen and Joan were just falling asleep when they heard a noise at their bedroom door. They were closing it now that Addison and Layne were back. Joan knew right away what the sound was. She got up and quietly opened the door.

Lizzie and Darcy entered and took their positions on the bed

Leveled in London

and they all slept soundly.

SCARLETT MOSS

Chapter Thirty

ALEN AND JOAN WERE AWAKED by a knock on their door. Alen opened the door. It was Addison.

"I'm sorry to wake you up. But I can't find Lizzy and Darcy anywhere! It's too early for the walker. I think someone stole my dogs!" she said in a panic.

Alen opened the door wider, put his finger to his lips, and pointed to the bed.

Addison stood there with her mouth open. She then silently whispered "thank you," turned and walked away.

Joan, who had remained frozen during the exchange, couldn't help it and let out a giggle. Then she got up.

"I better go see about Addison. I hope she's not mad," she said.

"I'll be right there too," Alen said. Then he looked at the dogs.

"And if you two know what's good for you, you better get up and go see your momma too. Some puppy dog eyes would go a long way right now," Alen said sternly to them.

Both dogs looked at him, then rolled over on their backs taking up the whole bed with paws in the air. Clearly, they weren't worried a bit.

"Addison, I'm so sorry. We didn't mean to scare you. They came to the door last night and were snorting under the crack and I let them in. That's where they've been sleeping since you left. I felt sure they weren't allowed in the bed. But we decided to adopt grandparent's rule."

"Oh, no! It's fine. I don't care. We tried to get them to sleep in the bed with us when we brought them home as puppies. And they wouldn't do it. They never have. I've just never walked in here in the morning that they didn't pop up and greet me. Except their one overnight at the vet when they were spayed and neutered. I'm sorry I woke you up. But where are the dogs now? Don't tell me they stayed in the bed?"

"Um, well, yeah. They play a game with us every morning. We have to do all the things to get them up in time for the walker. Do you want to play with us this morning?" Joan asked.

"No, this is clearly their thing with Aunt Joan and Uncle Alen. What I do want to do is video it. Do you mind? I won't share it with anyone, I know you're still in your pajamas," she asked.

"If you do want to share it, we have time to get dressed first. They don't get up until we play. No matter what. Well, except if the cops show up at the door."

While Joan and Alen drank coffee, Addison crept to their bedroom and took a few snapshots of the dogs snoozing in the bed on their backs. Then she went to her bedroom, woke Layne and told him what their fur children were up to, showing him the pictures.

She explained that the dogs had a game they played with Joan and Alen every day before they would get out of the bed and how on the first night Alen tried and tried to get them out of the bed. He wanted to see them with his own eyes, though he agreed to stay downstairs for the 'game' so as not to disrupt it and Addison could record it. Addison was thoroughly enjoying Joan and Alen and was in no hurry for them to leave. Except she was wondering…when they left, would Lizzie and Darcy go back to sleeping in the living room floor, would they start sleeping in Addison and Layne's bed, or would they continue sleeping in the guest room bed? As curious as she was, she knew she could wait to find out. There was so much fun to be had over the next few days.

The day went perfectly as planned. Alen hung out with Declan at the pub and spent the day cooking. The girls went to the spa. That night they went for an early dinner at The Ugly Shakespeare and swapped stories about their day. Addison noticed Declan motion subtlety to Layne. Layne excused himself, went to the restroom, and stopped at the bar to talk to Declan. It sure looked like the two were conspiring about something. And then she reminded herself about the production that would happen here tomorrow night and how seriously Declan took the whole thing and dismissed it.

"What's on the agenda for tomorrow? Other than Burns' Night, of course, I mean." Alen asked.

"Actually, I haven't told anyone, but I called Maisy Cooper," Grace said.

"Oh, how is she doing, the poor thing?" Joan asked.

"She's doing as well as can be expected. Lady Klara Pearce felt so badly that her niece killed Greyson that she has organized and is paying for a memorial service for him in the morning. But when I told her about your invitation to the palace, Maisy insisted on working with you tomorrow, to explain how it'll all go. She says she can have you curtsying like a born princess regardless of how nervous you might be. So, she wants to come to Addison's after the service. Is that okay with everyone?"

"What a delightful sounding lady. I would love to meet her," Addison said.

"Wow. That takes my breath away. She is worried about my silly event on the day she memorializes her son? The greatest loss of her life?"

"Well, like the Queen, she credits you with solving the murders of her son and her friend, River Read. If there was more time, she might have picked another day. But she said, that it will be nice to have something to do, some purpose after the service instead of going home to her one room and sitting there alone," Grace relayed.

"Then by all means, yes. I want to go Greyson's service. Do you know the time and place?"

"Yes, I agree. I want to go too," Grace said.

"I think we should all go," Addison said.

"She is a special lady. But while she's teaching you to curtsy, maybe I can come help Declan with the last-minute preparations?" Alen asked.

"No," all three women said at once.

"You need to learn the proper etiquette too. Maybe she can work with you first, then you can help Declan. I know you're enjoying this and that's wonderful. But Declan does this every year. Whenever you can come will be helpful to him," Grace said sternly.

"Yes, ma'am," Alen answered, and smiled sweetly at her.

~***~

The memorial service was beautiful with Lady Klara Pearce's orchids decorating the Wren Suite at St. Paul's Cathedral.

When they arrived, Maisy was in the ante-chamber called the beehive, receiving guests. She was delighted to see Grace and Joan and to meet the rest of the group. She whispered to Joan that she was nervous because Lady Pearce made such a fuss about planning the event and Maisy wasn't sure how many people would come. She need not have worried. There were seventy seats in the suite and all but three were filled. Maisy's minister performed the remembrance ceremony and afterwards tea was served in the beehive. Young people, friends of Greyson's from school and coworkers from the museum told Maisy stories about her son. She smiled through each one, listening and treasuring the stories she would try to hold on to in the coming days and years. Joan and Grace went to tell her goodbye. She told them she would come to Addison's as soon as it was over. They told her to take all the time she needed.

Addison made a phone call on the way home to Declan.

"I know you're busy today. But could you send lunch for seven to my house? We'll be home in about thirty minutes. Whatever is easy for you. Salad, sandwiches. Just something to last us until tonight."

"Thank you. Yes, of course. After lunch we will send Tommy and Layne and, as soon as he completes his lessons, Alen," she said smiling at the men in the group.

"Uh, I had plans…" Layne started to say.

"Don't even start with me, Layne Cotton. Your friend needs help," Addison admonished.

"But I can't cook," Tommy protested.

"He doesn't need you to cook. He needs help hanging decorations, moving tables, that sort of thing. You guys don't want to be there for Maisy's etiquette lessons, do you?"

"No!" they both said. And the matter was settled.

~***~

Maisy's lesson was complete, and she seemed to have fun working with Joan and Alen. Her lesson certainly put Joan more at ease about her audience. She learned to address the Queen as Your Majesty when they met and then ma'am, pronounced like jam, afterwards. Not to speak until spoken to. Not to touch the Queen, unless she initiated the touch. If Prince Phillip was there, to address him as sir. Not to turn her back to the Queen and not to leave until after the Queen left the room. Then she taught Alen how to bow from the neck as he should do when meeting the Queen. Alen left afterwards to go to the pub, where he was much more comfortable. While she was working with Alen, she requested that Joan put on the dress and shoes she would wear for the meeting.

Joan returned in her black and white plaid shirt dress with an asymmetrical flounced hem and her dressy black knee length boots with a moderate heel. Maisy proclaimed the outfit perfect and proceeded to show Joan first how not to curtsy. Then the proper way. She had her perform about thirty curtsies telling her that it would make it easier if she was nervous.

"I know she isn't your Queen, and you probably aren't nervous at all. But just in case," Maisy said.

"On the contrary. I am nervous. Sometimes I don't even want to go. No, she's not my Queen, but I don't want to reflect badly on Americans. I really appreciate you helping me. I'm sure avid royal watchers know all of this. I admit to being a casual royal watcher. You know the weddings, funerals, new babies. That's about it," Joan explained.

"It's my pleasure," Maisy said.

"I just had a thought. I know this has been a long and hard day for you Maisy. But tonight is Burns' Night and we're attending the celebration at our friend's pub down the street. Would you like to join us?" Addison asked.

"Thank you for the invitation. I haven't attended a Burns' Night since I worked in a pub to put Greyson through school." She paused. "Yes, thank you. I would love that very much," she answered. "Do I have time to go home and change into something more festive?"

"Yes, of course. We're all getting ready here. But meet us back here and we'll all go together," Addison said. The three friends were all standing in front of Maisy.

"Maisy, I know this is an American thing and not an English thing. But may we hug you? We are thankful for your help, we really like you, and we would like to comfort you now. If a hug is a comfort, we would be honored to give you one," Grace asked.

Maisy looked down at the floor momentarily, then looked back up. Her eyes were moist when she nodded yes. They resisted the urge to swallow her up in a good ole American group hug, and each one of them hugged her tight. Then Grace offered to drive her home and wait with her while she changed and bring her back.

"But you need to get ready too," Maisy said.

"Everything I need is in the car. I'll get ready at your flat if that's okay," Grace explained.

"Thank you. I think I'm going to like having American friends," she said and they all laughed.

SCARLETT MOSS

Chapter Thirty-One

BAGPIPES WERE PLAYING OUTSIDE THE pub. When they walked in, they loved the transformation. The tables where covered in tartan tablecloths. The centerpieces were brass lanterns with candles inside. At the bases were bouquets of thistle, heather, and pine tied with tartan ribbons. The napkins were adorned with paper napkin rings with a cameo of Robert Burns. Scottish flags hung from the rafters, and there was a large podium next to a square table. The front of the podium was covered in a poster-size image of Robert Burns. Inside *The Flower of Scotland,* the national anthem of Scotland, was playing. At each place setting was a printed program with Robert Burns on the outside. And Declan and a young man who could have been none other than his son were circulating in their kilts. Joan started snapping pictures as soon as they were shown to their table. It was set for ten after Addison made a hasty call to Declan after inviting Maisy. Joan looked to Maisy and discovered her cheeks were rosy and she was smiling, clearly enjoying herself. She was happy Addison thought to invite the woman.

Their table was at the front of the room closest to the podium, and Joan was surprised that the group of Americans would have the best seat in the house.

Inside the program, was Robert Burns' *Address to the Haggis* both as it was written in the Scottish dialect and translated into English. In the back of the program was another Burns poem entitled, *The Lass of Cessnock Banks*. Also translated into English. Drinks were served. Everyone was served a Bobby Burns cocktail that contained scotch, vermouth, and Benedictine with a splash of water.

Once all the seats were full, indicating everyone had arrived, the young man that looked like a young Declan approached the podium. He welcomed everyone to the event. The pipers moved inside and played as Declan carried out a large silver tray with a huge haggis on it. Joan knew from Alen's description they had prepared one huge haggis encased in a sheep's stomach for the address, and smaller individual haggis for serving. Declan Jr. began reading Burns' *Address to the Haggis*, and the Americans listened intently to the Scottish edition. They all knew they could read the English translation later.

Then dinner was served. A smoked haddock chowder began the meal, followed by haggis with neeps and tatties, (turnips and potatoes), and buttered leeks. It was a wonderful meal and a festive event. The dinner dishes were cleared and dessert, English Sticky Pudding, was served. But as the servers were delivering dessert to the tables, Declan approached the podium.

"Lasses and Lads, if I might have your attention. As many of you know, my family is descended from Robert Burns, and as such, this is our favorite night of the year. But this year, I would like to welcome some very special guests, all the way from the United States of America. Folks, stand up. Let's give them a round of applause."

Joan was so glad she'd splurged and they were wearing tartan.

"In this group is a very special lady. Her name is Joan Arny. Joan, with the help of her husband Alen, and friend Grace, helped solve the murder of our friend River Read, the murder of our friend Maisy's son, Greyson, an ongoing theft of a local museum, and exonerate all those the police were looking at who were innocent. So, tonight I dedicate the Burns poem *The Lass of Cessnock Banks* to Joan and declare her an honorary Scot."

Joan blushed and listened intently as he read it in Scottish and then quietly put her program in her purse for safekeeping, so she could read the English later. She was then given a standing ovation by the patrons of the event.

Alen handed Joan a small wrapped gift box. She opened it to find a crown charm to add to the bracelet he gave her in Scotland.

"You will always be my queen," he said to her as he kissed her and the room erupted in applause again.

It was a perfect evening. One that Alen and Joan would remember forever.

~***~

The next day the three couples went to Trafalgar Square to enjoy the biggest celebration of Chinese New Year in the world outside of China. The parade was magical, the music beautiful, the dancing exciting.

They ate Chinese food and failed miserably at trying to learn to say *happy new year* in Mandarin. There was a crowd of over one hundred thousand gathered for the event. It was loud and colorful. Everyone enjoyed the experience but were ready to get home at the end of the day. They ate dinner at Addison's for the first time since arriving. Leftovers from the Burns' Night celebration Declan sent home with them, and everyone went to bed early. Tomorrow was Alen and Joan's big day.

~***~

Tommy and Grace brought breakfast and were there to see them off. Today was also the day the shop was scheduled to re-open. They were taking the morning shift, while Addison and Layne would drive Alen and Joan to Buckingham Palace. They would wait for them after their meeting.

When they arrived, they discovered their audience was going to be in one of the rooms of the private residence. Joan was beginning to feel nervous. Alen had butterflies in his gut, but he was so proud of his bride, he never let it show. He provided support for her as she clutched his arm following the guard to the appointed room. They knew from Maisy's lesson that they would be shown to the room where they would wait for the Queen. They were to stand, only sitting if the Queen sat and invited them to do so.

They didn't have to wait long. Within a couple of minutes, the Queen entered through a door opposite the one Alen and Joan were shown into. She was dressed in a pink suit. Joan took a deep breath and waited until the Queen was in front of her, then she curtsied and Alen bowed. The Queen extended a gloved hand to Joan to shake hands.

"Welcome to Buckingham Palace," said the Queen.

"Thank you, Your Majesty," Joan answered.

"Please, let's have a seat and a chat," the Queen said as she turned and walked to her chair and indicated that Joan and Alen should sit on the sofa across from her. She asked Joan where she was from in the United States and what they had done while in London, besides solving crimes faster than the city police. Then she thanked Joan for being a lovely guest in the country and for helping to identify the thief and murderers.

"And where will you be going next on your house-sitting journey?" the Queen asked.

"We're going to Venice next, ma'am," Joan replied.

"Lovely. I shall alert them of your intended arrival," she said with a wink and a smile.

Joan smiled too while stifling a giggle. The Queen laughed indicating it was a joke and it was okay for Joan and Alen to laugh too. Then the Queen stood signaling the end of the visit, she shook both of their hands and bid them safe travels, then exited through the door where she came into the room. The guard saw them out of the palace where they returned to their waiting friends and the rest of their London experience.

The End

Click here to read Book 3 now:
https://www.amazon.com/dp/B084WLGR2S

Keep turning pages for links to the travel photo video and the book's recipes, links to the other books in the series, about the author and a message from Scarlett.

A message from Scarlett:

Hello, I know you have over a million choices of books to read. I can't tell you how much it means to me that you chose to spend some of your limited and valued reading time reading one of my books.

I truly appreciate it and hope I entertained you. If I did, I would appreciate a few more minutes of your time, if I may humbly ask, for you to leave a review for other readers who might be trying to select their next reading material.

If for any reason you were not satisfied with this book, let me know how I can do better by emailing me directly at

scarlett.moss@scarlettbraden.com.

The satisfaction of my readers and your feedback is important to me.

Hugs from Ecuador,

Scarlett

Leveled in London

Book 3 in the House Sitters Cozy Mysteries

Victimized in Venice

They escaped Edinburgh and London…what's waiting for them in Venice?

Venice: The City of Love;

Carnival: A decadent celebration of 'Game, Love, and Madness'

It's all fun, love, and frivolity…until someone ends up dead.

American House Sitters, Alen and Joan Arny are looking forward to exploring the most romantic (and dog-friendly) city in the world with a bulldog named Carina.

Now they wonder, is it possible to catch a killer with three million tourists in town…and everyone in costume?

Read *Victimized in Venice*, because we all love rooting for the underdog.

A clean cozy mystery. No graphic violence, sex, or strong language. Available in Large Print.

The House Sitters Cozy Mysteries will take you on adventures and land you in the middle of crimes in different international cities in each book. Enjoy travel photos and recipes from each destination along with charming dogs in each country. Look for corresponding journals. Each book can be read as a standalone and you can read them in any order

Click here to read now:

https://www.amazon.com/dp/B084WLGR2S

SCARLETT MOSS

Recipes

The following recipes are included in The House Sitters Cozy Mysteries Recipes, which you can find here: https://scarlettmoss.blogspot.com/

or at www.ScarlettMoss.com on the Recipes tab.

Mug Shot's Old Fashioned English Tea Loaf
Citrus Salad with Fried Roasemary & Olives
Mug Shot's Banana & Pecan English Pudding
Mug Shot's Bubblin Nut & Fruit Wich
Mug Shot's Cherry Pudding with Orange Custard
Mug Shot's Condensed Milk Pudding
Mug Shot's English Banoffee Pie
Mug Shot's English Toffee Cheesecake
Mug Shot's Mince Pie
Mug Shot's Raspberry Eton Mess
Mug Shot's Tea-Poached Dried Fruit
Roasted Squash & Couscous Salad with Toasted Pumpkin Seeds
Spinach & Squash Salad with Coconut Dressing
The Tea's Knees Blueberry Scones
The Tea's Knees Cinnamon Scones
The Tea's Knees Cranberry Cherry Scones
The Tea's Knees Glazed Lemon Creme Scones
The Tea's Knees Lavender Scones
The Tea's Knees Pumpkin Ginger with Sweet Tahini Glaze Scones
The Tea's Knees Strawberry Scones
The Ugly Shakespeare Chicken, Leek, Caerphilly & Prune Pie
The Ugly Shakespeare Beef & Guinness Pie

Leveled in London

The Ugly Shakespeare Beef Wellington
The Ugly Shakespeare British Baked Beans
The Ugly Shakespeare Hand-Raised Pork Pie
The Ugly Shakespeare Norwegian Haddock & Prawn Fish Pie
The Ugly Shakespeare Rabbit Pie
The Ugly Shakespeare Roasted Vegetable Winter Salad
The Ugly Shakespeare Shepherd's Pie
The Ugly Shakespeare Sticky Toffee Pudding
The Ugly Shakespeare Yorkshire Pudding
Warm Lemon & Rosemary Chicken Salad with Shallot Caper Dressing

Travel Photos

Joan's Travel photos of London are on the Scarlett Moss Cozy Mysteries Youtube channel:
https://www.youtube.com/watch?v=Aqm4Pq2R2Z4

Subscribe to the Youtube channel to be notified when new travel videos or book trailer videos are added.

(Keep turning pages for more stuffs!)

About the Author

Scarlett Moss is a pen name for Scarlett Braden's cozy mystery books. Scarlett also writes thrillers and poetry.

Originally from the southern United States, Scarlett now calls the Andes mountains of Ecuador home. She lives there with her husband and her Ecuadorian pound puppy, Picasso.

Scarlett found her writing voice and her passion for writing late in life and now it's her favorite thing to do, usually with Picasso, the writer's assistant, by her side or in her lap. She also enjoys the festivals and holidays of her adopted country.

If you would like to hang out with Scarlett, she would love to have you in her Facebook readers group called Scarlett's Cozy Couch: where you can get to know her better, enjoy her twisted sense of humor, and sometimes even win prizes. You can join here:

https://www.facebook.com/groups/ScarlettsSafeRoom/

If you just want to lurk and follow the progress of her cozy mystery books, you can follow the Scarlett Moss Facebook page here: https://www.facebook.com/ScarlettMossMysteries

Sign up for the cozy mystery newsletter to be informed when new books are released or sales are going on here:

bit.ly/CozyNewsletter